Destination: Bethlehem

Sharon Altman and Christine Winkelman
Illustrated by Amy Rosener

Destination: Bethlehem

Copyright © 2008

ISBN: 978-0-615-21800-7

by Sharon Altman and Christine Winkelman

Bella Maria Books
St. Paul, MN
bellamariabooks@comcast.net

Dedicated to

Pierson and Ethan

Advent is the time to awaken in our hearts
the expectation of he "who is, who was,
and who is to come."

REVELATION 1: 8

THANK YOU

This started with the two of us, a mother and daughter, embarking on a journey to write a book for the children in our lives. Thank you to those of you who have joined us at various points along the way: Matthew Altman, Kathy Buri, Lucy Cunningham, Janice Mahoney, Gabrielle Simons, Pam Wright, and Jane Ziebart who offered valuable critiques and insightful comments.

This story benefited from the help of many others through discussions on the manuscript and in focus groups: Corinne Able, Bjorn Amundson, Lisa Bekius, Robert Bogott, Kim Burns, Doug Smith, Karen Goulette, Rebecca Jacobi, Gail Kotoski, Kay Kromrey, Jan Ross, Therese Spaight, Stephanie Weber, Megan Westhoff, Heidi Young, and Cynthia Winkelman. We are grateful to each one of you.

Above all, thank you to our husbands, Dave and Ryan, who helped guide us in every direction during this journey. They gave us good judgment, encouragement, and patience.

With all this help, any mistakes remaining in the text must be attributed to the hungry, naughty donkey in this story.

How to Use Destination: Bethlehem

There are many destinations during the season of Advent: shopping malls, concerts, parties...but these can often bring a frantic emptiness to our lives. We hope this book helps you travel to the best destination of this season — Destination: Bethlehem.

The length of Advent varies, so we designed the book to have 24 chapters. If you begin to read the first chapter on December 1 and read a chapter a day, you will finish by Christmas. Each chapter is short enough to read aloud in 10 – 15 minutes; a time to unwind and re-focus on the true meaning of this season.

Optional Activity

Our children enjoy the tradition of opening up a small package each day that represents something from the chapter. For your convenience we have listed items you might already have in your home using toys and nativity set pieces; or items you could find at the grocery store. Place the nonperishable items in small bags or wrap with tissue paper and number the packages to correspond with the chapters. Watch the excitement in your children's eyes as they unwrap a package after each chapter.

1 — A small candle to represent the Messiah

2 — A shepherd statue to represent Zachariah

3 — Pistachios, a pear, or an orange

4 — An ornament for the Christmas tree

5 — A donkey statue from the nativity set

6 — Dates (make sure they're pitted)

7 — The Mary statue from the nativity set

8 — An item for the local food shelf or charity

9 — A bird ornament or another ornament

10 — A shepherd boy from the nativity set

13 — The Joseph statue from the nativity set

14 — A pomegranate

15 — A black toy horse or an ornament

16 — Balsam branch (off an evergreen tree)

17 — An ornament or a Roman soldier

18 — A camel statue from the nativity set

19 — Flat bread and hummus

20 — Crèche stable

21 — A candle - Jesus' birthday is almost here

22 — An empty manger, or straw excelsior

23 — Star or an angel from the nativity set

24 — Place baby Jesus in the manger

Table of Contents

1. Zachariah's Orchard

Jerusalem! Isaac squirmed and looked down at his feet as his friends began to talk about their travels to the Temple. He couldn't add anything to the conversation. His biggest regret was that he hadn't been there himself yet. He knew they didn't mean to make him feel badly when they asked their usual question: "Isaac, why haven't you gone to Jerusalem yet?" Isaac wanted to avoid the uncomfortable feeling he always felt when his friends asked that question so he slipped away from the group without their noticing.

Isaac was halfway up the hill just outside the town when he looked back. The boys were still talking and laughing. He turned and ran the rest of the way up to Zachariah's orchard. He often came there. It was a good place to think. Now he sat, perched on a sturdy branch, dangling one leg from the limb of a large fig tree.

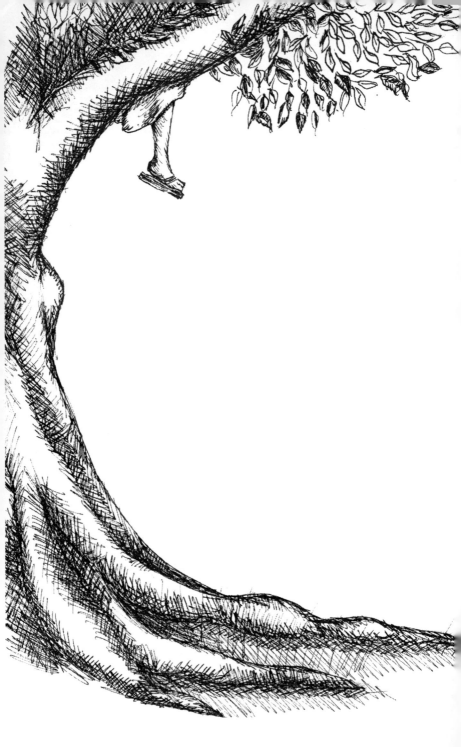

"I'm ten years old — going on eleven. I should have been to the Temple by now. It seems like there's always a reason I end up staying home — doing chores, or watching the younger ones. I'm glad so many people depend on me but when will it be my turn?"

Lost in thoughts, he didn't notice the old priest, Zachariah, standing next to the trunk, smiling up at him.

"Shalom, Isaac. You look upset today. What's bothering you?"

Isaac hopped down from the tree and told him about his wish to travel to Jerusalem.

Zachariah grinned, "You're young enough for your dreams to come true." His face changed as he went on, "At my age, you stop dreaming and think of all the things that could have been."

Isaac knew what he meant by this. Zachariah and his wife, Elizabeth had always wanted to have children of their own. Isaac opened his mouth to speak but stopped. There was nothing he could say. Zachariah was right. Everyone knew that now they were too old to have children.

Zachariah interrupted his thoughts. "Isaac, tomorrow's the day." Zachariah patted him on the shoulder. "Tomorrow you should talk to your father about going to Jerusalem."

Early the next morning Isaac woke to the sound of men talking outside and someone calling out Father's name. Isaac quietly tiptoed around his sleeping brothers and looked down from the bedroom window. Zachariah was talking to Father at the town well. Isaac ran down the stairs two at a time, bolting into the kitchen. "Good morning, Mother."

His mother stopped humming to his baby sister for a moment, "You're up bright and early!"

She handed him a warm piece of pita bread. Isaac took a big chomp and hurried out the door, colliding into Father and Zachariah as they were coming in. Father tousled Isaac's thick brown hair. The men paused for a moment to touch the doorpost, as they usually did, and said, "Hear, O Israel, the Lord our God, the Lord is One."

Now, Zachariah continued the conversation with Father. "Avner, I agree. We need to watch for the Messiah but the prophecies say someone must come first to prepare the people."

"You're right, Zachariah. But I wonder when that prophet is ever going to come?"

"We must not give up hope, Avner." Zachariah winked at Isaac. "This hope has no time limits — it goes beyond age."

The elderly priest looked at Avner. "Your son, Isaac, and I have been talking about hopes and dreams lately. He's young with many hopes and dreams. I'd like to grant one of them today."

Isaac's mind raced with excitement as Zachariah spoke. Today was the day Zachariah and the other priests from Ein Kerem would be leaving for Jerusalem to serve at the Temple.

Zachariah smiled at Father. "If it's all right with you, I'd like to bring Isaac along with me to Jerusalem."

Isaac's mouth dropped open in surprise and he looked at father for the approval. Father laughed as he nodded his head.

"Thank you, Father! And thank you, Zachariah!" Isaac shouted as he took off to tell his best friend, Oren, and the rest of the boys about his good news.

The day sped by. Before Isaac knew it, Mother and Father were hugging him good-bye, and it was time to leave. Isaac smiled broadly as Father patted his shoulder and told him, "You'll be sleeping in Jerusalem tonight... if all goes well and the donkey's fed."

Isaac always chuckled when Father said this. It was a family saying, one that Isaac was used to hearing often, but still thought was funny. He took off running to Zachariah's house.

Zachariah was waiting for him at the garden gate. Isaac gave the old man a hug. The elderly man's eyes lit up and he spoke slowly. "Isaac, today is a jewel in your life. Find a way to keep it and treasure it in your heart."

Once all of the priests were gathered outside at Zachariah's house, they began praying. Isaac eagerly joined them as they began reciting the psalm about going to Jerusalem, "I rejoiced when they said to me, 'Let us go unto the house of the Lord'..."

When the prayers were done, Zachariah paused as if he had something more to say. He began with a shaky voice, "I have a sense, an intuition that something is going to happen to me on this journey. I — I'm not sure quite what to expect." He stopped and rubbed his forehead with his thin hand. The other men circled around and encouraged him to trust the Lord. They each embraced the respected old priest and wished him peace, Shalom.

Then the group set out on the road to Jerusalem. As they hiked across the countryside, Isaac enjoyed every moment. Zachariah, who knew every hill and crossroad, answered all of Isaac's questions about where they were heading and told him stories about Jerusalem and the Temple. Isaac listened with growing excitement, imagining the beautiful city he was about to see.

It was nearly twilight when they climbed the last rise before the city and Isaac caught his first glimpse of Jerusalem. Zachariah pointed out the Temple and other landmarks outlined by the glow of burning lamps set in the windows of its ancient buildings. Jerusalem's gates were locked each day at sunset, long before the group had arrived, so they set up camp in a grassy valley a short way from the city. Later, at the campfire, the priests talked about what to expect when they reported for their duties at the Temple in the morning.

One of the priests, Sachi, talked about how last time they had come to Jerusalem he had just missed being chosen for the honor of entering the Holy of Holies. He hoped tomorrow it would be his turn. The other priests laughed and one called out, "You know that it all depends on which number is picked. We all have the same chance."

Sachi ignored them and continued, "Just think of how often I have come to serve at the Temple over the past fifteen years — more than thirty times! In all those years, I've never been assigned to burn the incense in the Holy of Holies. It's high time that I am the one to be picked. I've waited long enough!"

A man next to him nudged his elbow into Sachi's side and nodded his head in the direction of Zachariah, who had served much longer than Sachi but had never been chosen to go into the Holy of Holies. Isaac looked at Zachariah sitting next to him. The elderly priest was so humble, and Isaac never heard him complain.

Now, Zachariah stared into the flickering campfire and whispered a prayer so softly only Isaac heard it. "Lord, will it ever happen in my lifetime? Will I ever be chosen to serve in the Holy of Holies? I'm old and will be retiring soon — but I trust in You, Lord. Your will be done."

Zachariah noticed Isaac studying him. "We should never give up hope, Isaac." He thought for a moment and added, "Tomorrow will be a big day. Time to get some rest."

Little by little, the talking died down as everyone settled in for the night. Isaac was too excited to fall asleep right away. In the quiet of the darkness, he rested on his cloak, looking at the high stone wall surrounding the city. He thought about the stories Zachariah had told him about Jerusalem, and he couldn't help but wonder what it would be like to be in the Temple tomorrow. His busy thoughts gradually slowed down. Overcome by drowsiness, he drifted off to sleep.

Travel Guide
to the Past

• Jewish priests assumed their duties at the age of 20 and retired from active service at the age of 60. They were divided into twenty-four tribes. Zachariah and the other priests from Ein Kerem were from the eighth tribe, Abijah. Each priestly tribe was scheduled to serve in the Temple twice a year for one week at a time. The priests also served during the high festivals of Passover, Day of Atonement, and Pentecost.

• The Village of Ein Kerem is about five miles from Jerusalem. It is known to be the birthplace of John the Baptist.

• The door post of every Hebrew home had a small box containing a parchment with the beginning sentence of the first commandment, "Hear, O Israel, the Lord our God, the Lord is One."

2. THE JERUSALEM TEMPLE

IT WAS BARELY DAYLIGHT WHEN ISAAC'S dreams were interrupted by Zachariah's voice. "Isaac, Isaac, hurry or they'll leave without us!"

Isaac rubbed his eyes and looked around. The priests were already dressed in their white turbans and tunics for serving in the Temple. He jumped up as Zachariah handed him flat bread and dates to eat as everyone took off for the Temple together. Sachi began chanting a psalm, and the other priests joined in with rich, resonating voices. As they passed by the other campsites, people stopped what they were doing to stare at the group moving solemnly through the early morning fog. Isaac and the priests climbed higher and higher up the hill to the Holy City, leaving the fog behind. Their song ended as they arrived at the foot of the towering walls surrounding the city of Jerusalem.

"Shalom. Peace!" boomed a voice in the quiet of the morning. The city guard unlocked the heavy gate. "You are the first to enter at the Valley Gate today."

The group wound its way through the empty cobblestone streets, and before long they arrived at the massive stone stairs leading up to the Temple.

Isaac whispered, "Zachariah, there are so many steps!"

Zachariah leaned over and chuckled quietly, "The older I get, the higher these steps seem to become. I remind myself — go slowly and take one step at a time."

A loud wailing sound trumpeted from the Shofar. Isaac stopped and looked around to see where the sound was coming from. He spotted a man holding the shofar, high atop a platform. The man continued to blow the horn with long, vibrating notes that signaled the start of the day at the Temple.

The group came to immense wooden doors which were decorated with carved angels holding swords as if guarding the holy area beyond. Isaac had never seen such detailed woodworking. The angels' robes fell in graceful folds while their faces spoke of power.

As several priests slowly pushed the heavy doors open, Isaac took a deep breath — this was it! He was about to enter the Temple.

The Temple shone brilliantly. Isaac shaded his eyes as the rising sun glistened off the white marble walls and pillars surrounding a large courtyard. Isaac never imagined the Temple being this majestic. They passed through several large courtyards until at last they reached the rounded stairs that led into the Court of the Israelites. Isaac remembered his friends talking about this particular court which was set aside just for Israelite men to worship. He knew this was as far as he could go. He said a quick goodbye to Zachariah as the priests continued into the court where they would pray and offer sacrifices.

Isaac stood on his tiptoes so he could look over the wall encircling the priests' area. He watched Zachariah humbly whispering prayers as he and the other priests formed a circle around a temple official. This was the ritual the priests were talking about last night at the campfire: "The Casting of Lots".

The temple official removed Sachi's turban to show the selection process would begin with him. Sachi smiled broadly, nodding his head as he looked at the others. The temple official rolled precious gemstones to determine a number and began counting each man as he slowly walked around the circle to give work assignments for the day.

Jerusalem Temple Map

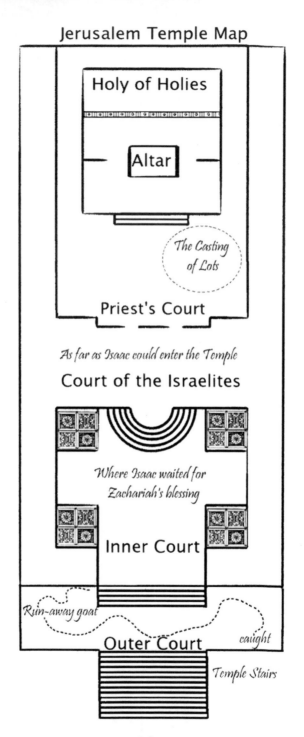

Holy of Holies

Altar

The Casting of Lots

Priest's Court

As far as Isaac could enter the Temple

Court of the Israelites

Where Isaac waited for Zachariah's blessing

Inner Court

Run-away goat

caught

Outer Court

Temple Stairs

When the official stopped at Zachariah, Isaac saw Sachi and the other priests gather around him, talking excitedly.

A few minutes later, Zachariah walked over to where Isaac stood. "I thought this dream of mine was hopeless, but today, at last, the Lord chose me for the honor of serving in the Holy of Holies!"

Isaac hugged Zachariah. "Oh, Zachariah, today is one of those days we both will treasure!"

Zachariah nodded, "Yes, Isaac." He then told Isaac the incense ceremony wouldn't take very long, and when he was finished he would stand at the top of the rounded stairs to give a blessing.

He warned Isaac, "Don't go too far if you want to get a good spot before the crowd gathers in the courtyard."

Isaac said, "Don't worry. I wouldn't miss that. I'll be there."

As Isaac was waiting, he heard a loud commotion coming from the outer courtyard. He glanced back and saw that Zachariah was still getting ready, so Isaac went over to investigate. He figured he wouldn't be gone for long.

The Outer Court was loud and crowded. The bleats of sheep and snorts of bulls blended together, making one loud chaotic hum. Isaac watched a man trying to lead a young, white goat through the crowd. The goat lowered its head, wiggled out of its rope, and ran away. Merchants gathered to help but the goat was fast and butted wildly, knocking open a crate of doves. The birds flew as the men chased after the goat. At last the men cornered the goat and slipped a looped rope back over its head.

Isaac had been so entertained watching the goat that he lost track of time. Now he began to panic as he remembered Zachariah's instructions to stand at the bottom of the round stairs to receive his blessing. Isaac turned quickly and wove his way back to the Court of the Israelites. By now a crowd had already gathered.

"Excuse me," Isaac said, as he squeezed his way through the sea of people until he came to the front of the court where he would be able to see Zachariah. Some of the bystanders chanted prayers with closed eyes while others occupied themselves in lively conversations about the Torah. Isaac stared at several men dressed in dark robes holding writing tablets. Zachariah had told him about these men. They were temple scribes, whose work was to write copies of Scripture.

Isaac stood patiently and waited, but it was taking Zachariah much longer than he had thought. After a while Isaac shifted from one foot to the other and began to wonder why Zachariah hadn't come out yet. People complained that the priest, Zachariah, was too slow. Isaac overheard a man question if something had gone wrong. Then someone gasped, "There he comes!"

Isaac saw Zachariah. His face was as pale as his white tunic. He took a few unsteady steps toward the staircase and swayed, leaning against the rail. Something was definitely wrong. Zachariah didn't stay at the top stair to give the blessing. He waved his arms at the crowd, shook his head, and began tottering.

The chattering crowd became eerily quiet as people realized something strange had happened to the old priest. The only sound in the whole courtyard was the tinkling of the bells on the edge of Zachariah's priestly robe.

Sachi rushed forward to help him down the stairs to a bench as Isaac ran over. Zachariah opened his mouth to talk but his voice was gone; not even a whisper came out. He moved his lips, but no one understood what he was trying to say. Zachariah rested his head in his trembling hands for a few minutes.

A deep voice in the crowd shouted, "Zachariah, what happened in there? Why can't you talk?"

Another voice added, "Get him something to write on!"

A scribe came over and loosened the small wax tablet that hung from his leather belt. He held onto Zachariah's arm and offered him the tablet. Zachariah nodded his appreciation for the tablet and began to write.

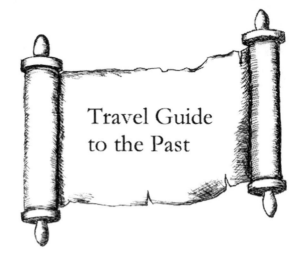

Travel Guide
to the Past

- The complicated process for assigning priests to various duties was called Casting Lots. It began with the priests standing in a circle; each priest holding up as many fingers as he decided. After a Temple official cast the lots (precious gemstones) to determine a number, the priests counted off around the circle until the determined number was reached. The first lot was for preparing the altar, the second for those who were to offer the sacrifice. The third lot, the most important, determined who was chosen to offer the incense in the Holy Place. Zachariah had waited most of his life before he had the honor of burning the incense in the Holy Place.

- A priest wore special garments for entering the Holy Place: a white linen tunic, a golden crown, a breastplate, and a robe edged with bells.

▪This is a blessing Jewish priests prayed:
May the Lord bless you and keep you.
May the Lord shine His face upon you.
May the Lord lift His countenance upon you,
And grant you peace. (Numbers 6:24-26)

▪ The Shofar is a trumpet-like instrument made from a wild goat's horn. It signaled the time to begin worship at the Temple and was also taken into battles.

▪ It took the strength of twenty men to open or close the massive Temple gates.

3. THE JERUSALEM MARKET

ZACHARIAH'S HANDS TREMBLED AS HE WROTE A message on the tablet. When the elderly man was finished, he carefully put it into a cloth bag, tied it shut, and handed it to Isaac. Zachariah rested his hands on Isaac's head for a wordless blessing. When he finished, he pointed in the direction of Ein Kerem. Even though Zachariah couldn't say anything, Isaac understood what he meant.

"Don't worry, Zachariah," he said patting the cloth bag. "I'll get this safely to Elizabeth. You can count on me."

Sachi interrupted. "I'm sorry none of us can go with you, Isaac. We, priests, have to stay in Jerusalem until the end of the feast. It's not safe for you to go by yourself but I know of some people leaving for home today. If you hurry, you can catch them at the Valley Gate."

Isaac remembered coming in through the Valley Gate that morning and was confident that he could find it all by himself. He said a quick good-bye to Zachariah and rushed out with the tablet.

Isaac ran down the Temple stairs into the city. The streets were crowded, much different than it was at dawn when they had entered the Holy City. He took off down a narrow street thinking it would lead to the Valley Gate, but the street turned and led him into the busy market-place. White canopies lined the street providing shade for stalls brimming with prickly pears and pomegranates, slices of honeycomb and slabs of cheese, bins of grapes and baskets of pistachios. The market was filled with the aroma of sweet incense and roasted meats. Tapestry merchants dressed in flowing robes and colorful turbans called out to the passing crowd in hopes of making a sale.

"Where is it?" Isaac muttered to himself as he kept looking.

He had to get to the gate where he would find his neighbors. The bustling crowd jostled Isaac along through winding cobblestone passages. There were too many people pushing, and everyone seemed to be nearly a foot taller than him. He hopped up and down a few times trying to see over their shoulders, but nothing looked familiar. Isaac passed two old women with weathered faces, sitting on pillows, guarding their large mounds of lemons and limes.

One of the women wagged her finger at him and cackled, "Little boy, we're watching you. Don't take our fruit without paying!"

Isaac began to explain, "I'm lost. I have to find the Valley Gate and…"

The woman stood up. "If you're not going to buy anything, move along."

He quickly turned away to follow a wealthy woman and her servant as they cut a path through the press of people.

"Ugh, ugh!" she grumbled clutching her delicate silk veil. "Keep these people away from me!"

She bumped a crate of doves. The birds became agitated and flapped their wings, sending feathers flying everywhere. Isaac watched one large, fluffy feather float high in the air and land softly on the head of the wealthy woman. She continued along with her chin pointed high, unaware of the ridiculous feather perched on her expensive veil.

Isaac giggled as the feather bobbed on the top of her head like a peacock's plume. He became separated from them as he was swept along, farther and farther from the gate where the people from Ein Kerem were preparing to leave.

"Where am I? Will I ever find the gate?"

He wanted to stop to get his bearings, but the sea of people kept moving him along. He thought his luck changed when he spotted a quiet passageway and made a quick turn to enter. A sense of danger set in as soon as he stepped into its shadow. Isaac had a strange feeling he was not alone. The skin on the back of his neck felt prickly; his legs felt wobbly. He saw them out of the corner of his eye: a band of boys who "owned" this alley. All of them were head and shoulders taller than him. The boys closed in, blocking his escape.

Isaac caught sight of a gray mouse running across the cracked cobblestones. He wished he could turn into a mouse now and run away too.

One of the boys snickered, "Hey Ebar, look what we trapped here."

Ebar was the leader. He was an ugly look-ing brute, heavily built, with lips that curled into a sneer. He stood boldly, hands on hips, glaring with an icy stare.

Ebar leaned into Isaac's face, "It looks like you're in the wrong alley, little mouse!"

The other boys circled around, howling like a pack of wild jackals, calling him names and grabbing at his clothes.

Ebar spoke again, "All right, stranger, since you're not from around here we'll give you a choice. You give us everything you have and then run away, or we beat you up, take everything from you and we run away. Which is it?"

Isaac didn't have money or anything else valuable. He wanted to tell them this, but he was too scared and couldn't get the words out. It didn't matter because the bullies didn't wait for an answer.

Ebar grabbed the sack with Zachariah's message and pushed Isaac to the ground. Isaac winced, feeling the full weight of Ebar's foot pushing him down. In one quick glance, Isaac saw the other boys pulling up their sleeves, clenching their fists. He closed his eyes and covered his head with his hands. Time seemed to stand still during these few seconds. Isaac felt sick with fright but he remembered a prayer he and his father often said together.

Deep within his heart he prayed silently, "In you, O Lord, I place my trust. Don't let my enemies win over me. I will not be afraid because you are with me."

He had a sense of reassurance. No matter what happened, he knew the Lord would be with him.

Travel Guide to the Past

- The small country of Israel was located at the heart of the ancient world. Jews traveled there from all parts of the known world to worship at the Temple. Merchants passed through Jerusalem on their way to Asia, Africa, or Europe. People of different cultures milled about the streets, shopping at the stalls which held a kaleidoscope of local and foreign fruits, vegetables, grains and household furnishings.

- The ancient Valley Gate was on the Western side of Jerusalem. It overlooked a valley of pastures for sheep and goat herds. The gate led into a busy market area populated by merchants traveling between Jerusalem and the seacoast town of Joppa.

- Isaac's prayer is based on Psalm 56.

4. An Alley in Jerusalem

Isaac crouched on the cobblestone alley, hardly daring to breathe, as he waited for the bully's first punch. The bullies grew silent, and then he heard a few new voices: men. Suddenly the alley exploded into a commotion of yelps and shouting all around him. He peeked through his fingers and saw several men waving broom sticks at Ebar and his gang. A feeling of relief swept over Isaac as he watched the men chase after the boys into the street.

Now the alley was quiet. He stood up and began walking toward the street when he felt a heavy hand on his shoulder. Isaac spun around and came eye to eye with a stranger. The first thing Isaac noticed was his big bushy eyebrows. The man's eyes darted around the alley to spot any bullies who may be still hiding in the shadows. Once satisfied that they were alone, the man asked in a deep voice, "What happened here?"

"I was lost and wandered into this alley. I didn't expect to get into trouble with those boys."

"They're a nasty bunch of bullys." The man explained, "I'm Harash. I own a store just down the street. The merchants around here are all too familiar with these trouble makers. They go around the market stealing goods from us. We were ready and followed them this time. It seems we rescued you just in time. This is a dangerous part of town as you now know!"

He looked closely at Isaac and asked, "How old are you?"

Isaac said shyly, "I'm going on ten and a half."

"Where's your guardian? You're too young to be wandering about Jerusalem by yourself."

Isaac explained how he came to Jerusalem with the priest, Zachariah, but when he began telling the story about Zachariah's loss of speech, Harash's face darkened.

Harash stroked his beard as he stared hard into Isaac's face. "That's a bunch of nonsense. Do you really expect me to believe such a story about one of our priests? Tell me the truth."

Behind him, Isaac heard the footsteps and heavy breathing of the other two merchants returning. Harash grabbed the collar of Isaac's tunic and spun him around to face the men, Omer and Simon. He pointed at Isaac and told them that they had just rescued a liar. Isaac's heart sank. His face became sticky with sweat as he looked at the men staring at him.

Omer studied Isaac. "This boy is shaking like a leaf. I've seen fibbers before, but this boy doesn't strike me as one. Look at his clear eyes and sincere face. I want to hear what he has to say for myself."

Simon tugged at his short brown beard. "Hmm. Why do you think this boy is lying, Harash? He has been through enough trouble today with the bullies. I'd be surprised if he would turn to outright lying now. Hmm."

Harash, annoyed that his companions questioned his opinion of Isaac, blustered impatiently, "Boy, tell them your ridiculous story. They'll find out, like I did, what kind of silliness you're making up."

Isaac took a breath and began slowly, "As I told you, it all began this morning when I went to the Temple with the priests."

He went on to tell them about Zachariah going into the Sanctuary and how he mysteriously couldn't speak when he came out.

Omer shook his head and exclaimed. "Harash, Harash. That's the news from the Temple everyone's been talking about today. We tried to tell you earlier, but you were too busy to stop and listen to us. If only your ears were as large as your belly, my friend, you'd be better off!"

Harash snorted, "Hah!," and patted his thick middle. "My belly is a sign of my wealth and success."

Simon smirked, "We are as wealthy as you, but we can still see our feet!"

Harash's angry face melted. He mopped his forehead and admitted, "Perhaps the boy told the truth."

He reluctantly offered Isaac an apology. "My friends are right — if I had listened to them earlier..."

Isaac smiled, "That's all right. It is hard to believe that Zachariah suddenly couldn't speak. No one knows why it happened, but I have the answer right here, on this tablet."

Isaac looked up to the sky and groaned, "Oh, no! The bully took it. The tablet is gone for good now! I'm supposed to deliver it to Ein Kerem."

Omer quickly spoke up. "When we caught the alley boys, I took a cloth sack from one of them." Triumphantly, he held out his hand with the sack still containing the precious tablet. "Those ruffians never had a chance to look inside."

Isaac gratefully took the sack and sank down exhausted onto an empty crate.

He sat with his eyes closed and his head leaned back onto a cool stone wall. He just wanted to sit there for a while, maybe for a long while, to rest.

Omer crossed his arms over is chest. "Well, we certainly took care of them. Those troublemakers won't be hanging around this alley anymore."

Simon laughed, "We gave them a good scare." His smile faded and he tugged on his beard. "There's still one more problem to solve. How are we going to get Isaac back to Ein Kerem?"

Omer suggested, "Perhaps he should go back to the Temple and find Zachariah."

Isaac quickly spoke up. "But I promised him that I would take this tablet to his wife, Elizabeth. I have to go to Ein Kerem today."

Harash's face lit up. "I have an idea: Matthew!"

The other two merchants nodded in agreement and said in unison, "Matthew."

Harash spoke up, "I know where to find him. You two can go back to your shops. I'll take care of Isaac."

Isaac asked, "Who's Matthew?"

Instead of answering, Harash reached down and pulled him to his feet. "Come on. Hurry, boy. We don't have much time. We've got to go now or my plan will never work."

That said, Harash led Isaac back into the bustling market.

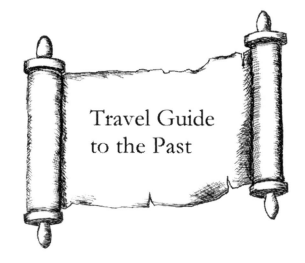

Travel Guide
to the Past

- Sacred Scripture does not elaborate on whether or not Zachariah sent a message to Elizabeth; however Luke 1:63 records that he used a tablet to convey an important message to his relatives.
- The kind of writing tablet that Zachariah may have used was made of wood that had a raised edge, forming a shallow box. It was covered with a thin wax covering. A pointed stylus was used to engrave a message onto the soft wax. To erase the writing, the surface could be pressed to re-smoothen for a new message. The modern expression, "a clean slate," comes from the "cleaning" of the wax tablet. Small wax tablets were easy and inexpensive to make and easy to carry. They were often fastened to a person's belt by a leather strap.

5. THE ROAD TO EIN KEREM

ISAAC HURRIED TO KEEP UP WITH HARASH AS HE puffed onward, threading his way through the noisy and confusing market. Isaac stayed close; he did not want to get lost again.

As they rushed along the passageways, Harash explained, "Matthew is a friend who is leaving Jerusalem this afternoon. He's taking his caravan west to the sea and will be passing very close to your village. It's the quickest way I can think of to get you home."

Isaac spotted a camel caravan just ahead. He had never been near a camel in his life but had always wished that someday he could ride on one.

"Camels! I can't believe today I'll be traveling in a caravan of camels!"

Harash was quick to correct him. "Oh, you're not traveling with that caravan. My friend, Matthew, has a caravan of ...donkeys."

Isaac tried to hide his disappointment about missing the chance to ride on a camel. He was thankful to be heading home, but he had never been fond of donkeys. He remembered the trouble he and his cousin, Jediah, once had trying to keep a stubborn old donkey on the path going up to Zachariah's and hoped these donkeys might be different.

Isaac followed Harash, continuing to stare back over his shoulder at the camels rather than watching where he was going. When Harash came to a sudden stop, Isaac ran right into his back.

Harash put his large hand to his lips. "Shhh. Let's play a joke on my friend, Matthew."

"Where is he?" asked Isaac.

"He's right over there," Harash pointed.

Isaac looked around Harash's broad shoulders to see a tall young man holding a basin of water; and three scruffy looking donkeys surrounded by baskets filled with merchandise.

Matthew spoke in a soothing voice, "Sil, my good little donkey, let's soak your hoof. There, there girl, I'll take good care of you. I wish you could tell me what happened and how..."

Harash crept up and interrupted in a deep voice, "Master, thank you for taking such good care of my hoof."

Matthew jumped up, startled by the voice. The basin of water spilled all over his sandals and ran down the cobblestones. Harash burst out laughing, his belly rolling with each chuckle.

Matthew shook his head and groaned, "Harash. I should have known. You're always making fun of me and my animals. I've told you many times, these donkeys are noble creatures."

Harash rocked back and forth, still laughing and spluttered, "Give me one reason to believe donkeys are noble!"

Isaac had been standing off to the side, listening to Harash and Matthew, but now stepped forward and spoke. "I've studied the Torah with my father, and learned that some of our greatest kings: Saul, David and Solomon all rode on donkeys. You can't get much nobler than that."

Matthew raised his eyebrows and looked at Isaac, "A good reply." He turned to Harash and asked, "Who is this young scholar?"

"This boy, Isaac, needs to get to Ein Kerem. I was hoping he could travel with you."

Matthew replied, "I could use his help and I'd enjoy the company of someone who knows about our heritage." Turning to Isaac, he tossed him a large cloth, "How are you with donkeys?"

Isaac caught the cloth and bent down to dry Sil's hoof. He looked up and saw Harash already hurrying back to the marketplace.

"Thanks, Harash," Isaac called out to him. Harash turned his head and waved to Isaac, as he continued on his way.

Isaac helped Matthew feed the donkeys and load the animals with packs of merchandise.

"Matthew," Isaac asked, as he stroked the little donkey's neck, "what's the matter with Sil?"

"This morning, when I cleaned dung from her front hoof, I found a pebble had bruised her foot. She already started to develop an infection, so I'm worried. I can't allow my good animals to become lame. She'll need to take it easy, so we'll keep an eye on her."

The little donkey twitched her fuzzy ears as if she understood.

As they began the journey, Matthew handed Isaac a walking stick and reassured him, "You'll be back in Ein Kerem before evening meal."

Isaac smiled and added, "If all goes well and the donkey's fed."

Matthew stopped and stared at him with a blank look. "Uhm — I don't get it. You just helped me feed all of them."

Isaac laughed and began to explain, "It's something my family always says before leaving on a journey. I guess it's just a habit. Many years ago, when my father and his brother, Levi, were youngsters, they learned an important lesson: When traveling, no matter how tired you are, the donkey needs to be fed."

Matthew laughed, "Uh-oh. I can see where this story is going. Hungry donkeys can get into plenty of mischief."

Isaac nodded and went on. "Well, they were too tired to feed their donkey, and while they were sleeping he ate all their honey cakes and bit a hole in their water pouch. When they woke they had no food, the water pouch was empty, and their donkey was gone. They searched all day, and finally found him in a neighboring town, eating the rabbi's roses. Their older brothers teased them for months about their foolishness, and out of that came this saying. I guess it stuck."

"It sounds like your father and Levi had quite an adventure. Do they still do things together?"

Isaac said, "Well, no — not any more."

He hung his head and kicked a small stone. "A few years ago, Levi and his family moved far away to Zippori, where he could find steady work as a carpenter. Zippori is a long way from Ein Kerem. I miss them — especially my cousin, Jediah."

Matthew and Isaac continued talking as they headed west over the grassy hills of Judea. The warmth of the sun brought out a swarm of flies that hovered and buzzed around the donkeys.

Isaac and Matthew did their best to swat the pesky insects away; however, the bothersome flies bit Kita, another one of Matthew's donkeys.

She was wild, headstrong, and voiced her protest in a constant chorus of brays. "Haw — He —Haw." She twitched her ears and flicked her tail to get rid of the annoying flies. At last she sat down, and rolled in the dirt. Packs loosened and fell off all over the road. Matthew and Isaac yanked and coaxed but couldn't get the stubborn donkey up.

Meanwhile, the smell of the sweet grass was too tantalizing for Matthew's plump little donkey, Bishra. He tugged on his line until the knot loosened. Now free, the fuzzy brown donkey headed off on his own, munching tender blades of grass.

"Isaac, would you go get Bishra while I deal with the other two?"

Isaac caught up with the donkey grazing contentedly out in a field. He held out a handful of fresh, green clover as a bribe to lead him back to the road.

When they joined the other donkeys, Isaac fed Bishra another clump of clover and told him, "I know how you feel, Bishra. My stomach is growling."

Matthew overheard him. "So you're hungry."

"I'm so hungry even the clover looks good."

Matthew opened a saddle bag and pulled out a large chunk of bread and a slab of cheese for him. Isaac took a big bite of the bread and mumbled with his mouth full, "Thanks."

They set off again toward Ein Kerem. The sun was now low in the sky, making their shadows long enough to reach the edge of the road. The donkeys clip-clopped onward without any further ruckus.

Matthew and Isaac talked about many things along the way, but as they neared the last hill leading up to Elizabeth's house, Isaac became quiet. With each step he tried to think of a way to tell her about Zachariah's mysterious loss of speech without worrying her.

Matthew noticed the change in Isaac and asked what was bothering him. After listening to Isaac's concerns, he encouraged him saying, "You'll know what to say when you see your friend, Elizabeth. Trust in the Lord; he will help you."

Isaac nodded, but the dreaded job of bringing the bad news to Elizabeth hung over him like a dark cloud. He clutched the sack with Zachariah's message tighter, wondering what he would or could say to her. It wasn't going to be easy.

Travel Guide
to the Past

• When he was five years old, Isaac would have begun studying Torah, the part of the Bible known by Christians as the Old Testament. Children at this age would memorize large portions of Scripture and would eventually know the entire Torah by memory. At ten years, they began learning the Mishnah (the interpretations of Scripture). When they were thirteen, boys and girls studied the commandments; and at fifteen, studied the Talmud (Jewish ethics, customs, and history).

• Isaac's journey from Jerusalem to Ein Kerem was about five miles over the hilly grasslands, westward towards the Mediterranean Sea.

6. Arrival in Ein Kerem

Isaac and Matthew tapped their walking sticks on the road coaxing the little fuzzy donkeys to trot up the last hill. They were nearly at the end of the journey. Looking ahead, they saw Elizabeth, her hand shading her brow, peering anxiously toward Jerusalem. She had already heard bits and pieces about Zachariah from the villagers who returned earlier that day. She hurried past her garden and met them just as they reached the yard. Huffing and puffing, she dabbed her teary eyes.

Elizabeth began to ask them, "Where's Zachariah?" but noticing their long tired faces, changed her mind and asked, "Please, Isaac, won't you and your friend come in?"

Elizabeth was known for her hospitality to friends and visitors. She quickly brought a large jar filled with fresh water from the well and gave Isaac and Matthew drinks. Then she filled a wide basin with the rest of the water and offered each of the weary travelers a fresh towel.

"I thought you'd like to wash up before eating."

Isaac and Matthew grinned and nodded. The water was soothing, and they appreciated the chance to clean their hands and wash the dust off their feet.

Meanwhile, Elizabeth went into the kitchen and filled a plate full of red pomegranates, dates and warm honey cakes. She dished up bowls of steaming lentil stew as they sat down to eat.

After dinner, Isaac handed Elizabeth the cloth sack containing the wax tablet and explained that Zachariah had written a message on it. Elizabeth carefully opened the sack and took out the tablet. She began reading it to herself but looked up to see Isaac and Matthew staring at her.

"I can see you two are wondering what he wrote. I'll read the message out loud for you.

After lighting the incense, I looked up and became frightened; I was not alone. I peered into the rising smoke and saw a heavenly angel standing in front of me.

He said, "Do not be afraid, Zachariah, because your prayer has been heard. Your wife, Elizabeth, will bear you a son and you shall name him 'John.' He will be filled with the Holy Spirit even before he is born and when he gets older, he will teach many people about the Lord."

I said to the angel, "How can I be sure this is true? Elizabeth and I are so old."

The angel frowned and spoke sternly.

"I am Gabriel. I stand in the presence of God. He sent me to bring you this good news but since you don't believe what I said, you will not be able to talk until these things take place and John is born."

~ And in a flash, the angel disappeared.

When Elizabeth stopped reading, she gently placed the tablet on the table and sat very still, hands folded on her lap.

"So our prayers have been heard, after all these years. Zachariah often said, 'Children are the true riches of one's life.' And now we will have a son even in our old age!"

Isaac and Matthew sat dumbfounded. They looked at each other with raised eyebrows and then stared at Elizabeth wondering how she could believe this was true. Neither said anything, hesitant to voice any doubts after hearing what happened to Zachariah when he questioned the angel.

After a long period of awkward silence, Matthew cleared his throat, "Ahem — Well, I think I'd better check on my donkeys." He excused himself and Isaac slipped out with him.

Elizabeth could tell by the way they looked at each other they didn't believe Zachariah's message. When they came back to the house, Matthew told Elizabeth, "Sil's leg is too sore for her to travel with me to the seaport, Joppa. Is there any chance that she could stay here until I return?"

Elizabeth agreed to stable Matthew's injured donkey in their barn.

Isaac promised, "I'll come up here every day to help take care of Sil."

Elizabeth smiled. "I'm glad we can count on you, Isaac."

After Sil was settled in the snug barn, Isaac and Matthew hurried along the road to the village. Isaac was excited to have Matthew stay at his house before he left for Joppa the next morning.

In a few days, Zachariah and the other priests were finished serving at the Temple and returned home. Isaac was taking care of the donkey and saw Zachariah walk up to the house where Elizabeth stood to greet him. Zachariah moved his lips to say something, but not a sound came out of his mouth.

Elizabeth's eyes widened. "Oh my! So it is true!"

Zachariah shrugged his shoulders, shook his head, and shuffled inside the house. Isaac fed Sil and went home without going into the house that day. The silence was so strange. Zachariah and Elizabeth usually talked about everything.

That evening, the old couple sat together in the light of a flickering lantern. Elizabeth turned to Zachariah and gently kissed his wrinkly cheek. Then she recited aloud the prayer he usually said in the evening:

"Blessed are you, the Most High God of Israel.

Even though darkness covers the earth we look for the light of dawn to come.

And though we have troubles, we trust in you, Lord, to watch over us.

Lord, you show us your tender mercy and we will rest confidently in your promises."

It grew late; the lantern dimmed and went dark. The old couple held each other's hands, quietly listening to the leaves rustle outside in the warm breeze. God's peace surrounded them and strengthened their marriage with a special tenderness for each other.

Days passed by, then weeks; Elizabeth recognized the signs that she was indeed expecting a baby. After a while, the couple kept to themselves around home, away from the questions of nosy neighbors. They looked after each other. Zachariah often helped Elizabeth with daily tasks as they became more difficult for her.

Isaac came every day to feed and brush Sil. Whenever the little donkey heard Isaac open the gate to the yard she brayed, "Haw — He — Haw." Elizabeth would look out the window to wave at Isaac and laugh at the little donkey.

One day, Elizabeth heard Sil bray and looked out to see Matthew, the merchant, returning from his business travels. He was pleased to see his donkey's hoof had healed up quite well. Sil was healthy and even a little fat. He also noticed that the message, given to Zachariah by the angel, was coming true. It had become obvious Elizabeth was expecting a baby.

Matthew clasped Zachariah's hands, "Mazel Tov. Congratulations on the Lord's blessings. May he continue to watch over and protect you."

Zachariah smiled with closed lips. The old couple waved good-bye to Matthew and watched him lead his donkey down the dirt path. As they turned back toward home, Elizabeth stopped short. She answered Zachariah's concerned look.

"Don't worry. The baby and I are fine, but all of a sudden I had a feeling, a sense that someone special would be coming to stay with us. I'm not quite sure who it will be or when the visitor will come, but I feel that it might be soon. I think I'd better get the house ready."

Travel Guide
to the Past

- Zachariah and Elizabeth were considered to be "well along in years." (Luke 1:7)   In their culture, it meant that they were at least sixty years old — many years past the age a woman would be able to have a baby. It was a miracle for elderly Elizabeth to become pregnant.

- Zachariah's evening prayer is found in the writings of the prophet Isaiah 60:1-2. This part of Isaiah's book contains many references about the promised Messiah.

7. THE VILLAGE OF EIN KEREM

FEW VISITORS EVER CAME TO EIN KEREM, so when Isaac heard people talking about a small group of travelers from Galilee who had stopped at the edge of the village, he ran to see who it was, hoping his cousin Jediah had come to visit. When he got there all he saw was a young woman. She was standing in the olive grove talking to Chloe, the town weaver. Chloe was pointing with an outstretched arm, giving the mysterious visitor directions. When she noticed Isaac, she called him over.

"This young woman is trying to find Zachariah and Elizabeth." Chloe stopped and turned to look at the woman again. "What did you say your name was?"

"Mary."

"Ah yes, Mary. This is Isaac. He goes to see Zachariah often."

Looking back to Isaac, Chloe fluttered her hand to swoosh him along. "You'll make sure Mary gets there, won't you Isaac?"

Isaac agreed and Chloe nodded as she turned to go back to her house. He took a closer look at the stranger and wondered if she may be the guest Elizabeth was expecting. She was dressed in traveling clothes; a simple woven tunic and cloak touched her feet in gentle gathers. A white veil held back her thick black hair except for one strand that slipped out and curled towards her cheek. Isaac picked up her travel sack and led the way.

Mary thanked him. As they walked through town, curious neighbors looked out of their houses, whispering to each other about the stranger. Mary met each of their stares with a gentle smile and a softly spoken, "Shalom."

Half way up the hill, past the vineyards, Mary's steps quickened. Running ahead, she waved and called out, "Shalom, Cousin Elizabeth!"

Elizabeth, who was now six months pregnant, was coming down the hill to meet them. She stepped gingerly along the winding path with hands on the small of her back. When the two women met, they held each other and pressed their cheeks together. Suddenly Elizabeth jerked and pulled away. She looked intently at Mary, "Blessed are you among all women and blessed is the baby you are carrying within you!"

Isaac looked again at the young woman. He could certainly not tell she was pregnant. How did Elizabeth know this?

Elizabeth continued, "Why am I honored with a visit from the mother of my Lord?"

Isaac wondered if Elizabeth knew what she was talking about. Could she really mean that this girl would be the mother of the Messiah? His mouth dropped open and he stared at Elizabeth as her greeting went on.

"When I heard your voice, the baby within me leaped for joy." Elizabeth smiled at Mary and leaned in to whisper, "And you — you are blessed because you have believed the things the Lord told you will come true." She winked at Mary, as if there was a secret only she and Mary knew.

The two women walked arm in arm talking and laughing on their way back to the house. Isaac followed behind. He overheard Mary talking excitedly, speaking the words of Scripture to praise God. When they came near the house, Zachariah came out, giving Mary a warm smile. She spoke gentle words of encouragement to him. Zachariah, still unable to speak, nodded and brought her inside to get settled. Mary said she would like to stay to help until after their baby was born.

Isaac was fascinated by this visitor and wished someone would tell him more about her, but everyone was too busy to explain. He decided that somehow he had to find out about Mary.

Just before dusk, Isaac carried a supper basket to the orchard for Zachariah, Elizabeth and Mary. They spread a blanket to sit on under a tree, and Zachariah propped a big plump pillow against its trunk. He took Elizabeth's arm and helped her get settled down onto it.

As Isaac began walking away, he heard Mary start to describe something wonderful she had experienced. He knew he really shouldn't, but he climbed up a ladder into a nearby tree to listen.

Perched on a low branch, partly hidden behind the leaves, Isaac strained to hear her. He cupped a hand around his ear and leaned forward.

Mary said she was at home in Nazareth when it all began. There was a brilliant light and she saw a heavenly figure in its brightness.

Isaac jolted upright. This sounded just like what had happened to Zachariah when he saw an angel in the Temple. His mind raced and he gasped, "Another angel messenger? How could this be?"

Before he knew it, his leg slipped and he lost his balance sideways on the tree branch. He desperately hung onto it until his hands slipped and he fell with a thud onto the soft soil.

At first, the three adults were startled. After a few seconds, Elizabeth held back a chuckle while Zachariah looked at him sternly. Isaac got up and hung his head. He kicked a stone as he said, "I'm sorry. It was wrong to hide and listen in on you."

Mary turned to Isaac with a gentle expression. Her deep brown eyes seemed to look right into his heart. "Isaac, since you've already heard part of the story, I'm sure you would like to hear the rest of it."

Although Isaac was utterly embarrassed, he was even more curious to hear what else she had to say about the angel. He sat down quietly along the edge of the blanket.

Mary continued, "The angel began by telling me I was favored by God. I was confused, a little upset and scared. Why was he telling me this? After all, I'm just like any other girl from Galilee. When the angel spoke again, it was almost as though he knew my thoughts. He said, 'Do not be afraid, Mary.' I tried to collect myself and calm down, but then he told me something even more astounding. 'You are going to have a baby boy. His name will be Jesus because he will be the Son of God and he will save his people.'"

Mary glanced over at Isaac and paused for a moment. She could see by his face that he was trying to sort out what she was saying.

"I remember that at the time, my mind felt like it was spinning. I turned my head a little toward the angel as I raised my veil and spoke with him. I wondered how I was to have a baby since Joseph and I were not yet husband and wife. But the angel assured me that the Holy Spirit would make all of these things possible. He said, 'With God, nothing is impossible.' And I believed him. I said, 'Yes… Let it happen just as you say.' At that moment I felt a faint breeze — a gentle puff of air, soft as the fluttering of a dove's wing, but I knew its presence was real — unmistakable. It surrounded me and whispered within my heart, 'My beloved, receive my life.' A great peace came upon me."

Mary's face was radiant with joy. She turned to Elizabeth. "Just before he left, the angel told me you and Zachariah were expecting a baby. From that moment I could hardly wait to come and help you."

Elizabeth wrapped her arms around Mary and beamed with joy.

Isaac listened the whole time without saying a word and when Mary finished talking, he got up from the blanket. It was time to go home. While he said good night to Elizabeth, she pulled him towards her to give him a big hug. Zachariah nodded and patted him on the shoulder. Mary smiled and said, "Erev Tov, Isaac, peaceful evening to you."

Isaac smiled shyly at Mary and scratched his head, trying to make some sense out of what he had just heard. As he walked along the dirt path back to his house, his mind was flooded with hundreds of questions. He wondered about the angel messengers who came to Zachariah and Mary. He wondered why Mary was chosen and if what she said could possibly be true. Could her baby be the Savior promised to Israel? He felt a little disappointed in himself as he thought about how hard it was, sometimes, for him to believe. Isaac wished he could have faith to trust God right away, like Mary. As he neared his home, he prayed, "Please, Lord, help me to believe the angel's amazing message."

Travel Guide
to the Past

- The conversation between Mary and Elizabeth is found in the Gospel of Luke.
- The exultant leaping of Elizabeth's baby reminds many people of the jubilant dancing of King David in front of the Ark of the Covenant in Jerusalem. Both Mary and the Arc of the Covenant carried something important. Mary held within her the Messiah, the promise for the future. The Ark of the Covenant held several sacred items from the Jewish past.
- The Holy Spirit overshadowed Mary when she said, "Yes." Writers of Sacred Scripture use images such as a dove or a gentle breeze to portray the person of the Holy Spirit.
- Mary stayed with Zachariah and Elizabeth for about six months. It was customary for women to help each other weave and sew swaddling cloths, blankets, and clothing in preparation for the baby's birth.

8. ZACHARIAH AND ELIZABETH'S HOUSE

ISAAC LOOKED AT THE SWADDLING CLOTH stretched out on a long mat inside Zachariah and Elizabeth's house. The narrow strip of white fabric was no wider than his hand. Next to it sat a basket filled with sewing needles and thread that Elizabeth and Mary were using to decorate it. He bent closer to examine the patterns sewn on the fabric. Each stitch was perfect. He recognized the row of symbols from Zachariah's priestly robes but these designs were tinier and even more colorful: red, blue, green, but the golden yellow — that was Isaac's favorite. He could just imagine this beautiful swaddling cloth snugly wrapped around the baby.

Mary and Elizabeth had been busy during the past few months. Isaac looked around the room noticing even more of their handiwork. There was a tall pile of soft, hooded baby coverlets and baby blankets near the door.

He asked Elizabeth, "How many things does one little baby need?"

She chuckled. "We made more than we need so we could share our joy with others. Isaac, would you help Mary bring the extra blankets to the village?"

Isaac brought a small wooden cart to the house, and Mary lined it with a fresh white linen cloth. They loaded the cart with baby blankets and shawls until it was brimming full.

As they walked down the hill to the village, Mary sang a joyful song that Isaac often heard her sing with Elizabeth.

*"My soul sings of the glory of the Lord
and my spirit rejoices in God, who is my Savior.
He has looked with kindness on me, his faithful servant.
Because He has honored me, future generations will bless me.
He is always merciful to those who love and obey him,
but He humbles the proud hearted.
He feeds the hungry, but he gives nothing to the greedy.
The Lord has done great things for his people.
Holy is his name."*

Isaac recognized these Scripture verses spoken at the synagogue but he had never heard them woven together in such a lovely way before. He asked Mary how she came up with this song.

Mary thought a moment, "Well, Isaac, the Lord has been doing so many wonderful things that this prayer of praise practically tumbles out. Have you ever experienced God's kindness and help?"

Isaac told her, "I ran into trouble with a gang of boys in Jerusalem. Just when it looked hopeless, I prayed. The next thing I knew the boys were chased away by merchants and I was rescued."

Mary smiled, "The Lord is always with us — even in the darkest places. Isaac, you and I each have reasons to praise the great kindness of the Lord and to thank him."

Isaac nodded in agreement.

The first house they came to in the village belonged to a poor family. Isaac knew that many of the villagers avoided these people, but that didn't make any difference to Mary. A pregnant woman, Judith, greeted them. Isaac played with her children while the two women sat down in the shade next to the herb garden. It didn't take long before the women were talking like old friends.

When they were getting ready to leave, Isaac heard Mary ask Judith, "Would you give us a handful of basil and onions in exchange for a baby blanket? Your garden looks so healthy and the herbs would give our stew a wonderful flavor tonight."

Isaac wrinkled his forehead and looked at Mary quizzically. He knew Elizabeth had a large herb garden of her own and certainly didn't need herbs from anyone. Mary turned to him holding her finger to her lips and gave him a knowing look. She turned back to Judith who was already cutting the basil while Isaac ran to the cart and returned with a baby blanket and a small hooded shawl to give the woman.

They spent the rest of the day going throughout the village, stopping to visit at various households. Isaac was surprised how many baby blankets they were able to give away. He knew the villagers wouldn't accept a gift without giving something in return. He admired the way Mary traded with them. Through her conversations, she found each woman's talents and came up with clever ways to acknowledge their skills, while giving them the blankets they needed. By the end of the afternoon, a peaceful joy rested throughout the town.

Isaac's cart was emptied of blankets but full of a variety of things from each family they had visited: the fresh herbs from Judith's garden; a blue cloth, large enough for a veil, woven by Chloe; a basket of juicy berries, a plump feather pillow, and a pottery jar filled with olive oil from others.

As they walked back up the hill, Mary told Isaac, "My heart feels like a bubbling brook — it's so full of joy. The time for Elizabeth's baby is almost here. The child growing near her heart is just the beginning. Very soon everything is going to change."

Isaac walked on with Mary in silence, wondering what change she was talking about.

A few days later, Elizabeth delivered a healthy baby boy. The new parents' hearts nearly burst with love for their baby. Elizabeth talked and cooed to the baby; however, Zachariah was still unable to speak a single word.

Eight days later, they went to the synagogue to announce their baby's name. Elizabeth nervously played with the edges of John's blanket. She hoped yesterday's argument with family and friends about the name "John" would not come up again. Everyone told her the baby ought to be named after his father, but Elizabeth knew what the angel had told Zachariah.

She insisted, "He will be called John."

But now the argument began again and grew louder. They told her she was going against tradition; no one in their family had that name.

The discussion stopped abruptly when Zachariah stepped forward and placed the wax writing tablet on the table with a thud to get their attention. The room went silent. He pointed to the tablet and gestured for them to come closer. They leaned in to see the words:

His name is John.

Zachariah tenderly picked up his baby, John, and held him in the crook of his arm. Next, something amazing happened. Zachariah beamed with joy and began speaking.

"The Lord has answered my prayers. He has given us a son — the child we've hoped for throughout our marriage."

Everyone was shocked that Zachariah regained his speech. Many had assumed that he would never talk again. After a moment's pause, some guests turned to each other with questions, others shouted with joy. Zachariah held up his hand to quiet them.

"There's more I want to say. During these past nine months, the Lord has given me a vision for this child." He looked at baby John and spoke in a hushed tone, "You, my child, shall be a prophet of the Most High. Someday you will teach the people about the Lord's faithful love. You will be the one who prepares the way for the Messiah."

Zachariah handed the baby to Elizabeth and raised his arms to pray a blessing over the guests circled around him.

"The time is near for the Lord God of Israel to save us from our enemies; to free us so we can worship him fearlessly all the days of our life. The dawn of a new era is upon us. We, who are dwelling in darkness, shall see a great light!"

They all went back to Zachariah and Elizabeth's house to celebrate. Music and dancing began, laughter and talking broke out, and everyone was filled with joy. After a while, baby John grew sleepy and Elizabeth put him into the crib. Isaac came closer to look just as John opened his mouth in a big yawn showing his tiny pink tongue. Isaac smiled, quietly thinking about what words that little tongue would someday say about the Messiah. His thoughts wandered, recalling the marvelous events that had taken place over the past months. He hoped the story about Zachariah, Elizabeth, and John would be retold again and again so it would be remembered for many generations to come.

John slept on, having no idea an angel had been sent to announce his birth or that someday he would be called "The Baptist" and be the one to baptize the Messiah; having no idea that people would come from far and wide to hear him preach, or that one day even the King of Judea would listen to what he had to say.

Isaac looked up from the sleeping baby at Elizabeth. She smiled at him, brushing a strand of silver hair from her face, and said, "Isaac, now that the baby is born, Mary will be leaving soon. I know she'd like to say goodbye to you."

Isaac answered, "I like Mary. I wish she didn't have to go."

"We're all fond of Mary and will miss her, but it's time for her to begin a new life. She'll be marrying Joseph. He's a carpenter in Nazareth."

Isaac brightened. "Nazareth! That's only a few miles from Zippori where my cousin, Jediah, lives. You remember him, don't you, Elizabeth?" Isaac added sadly, "He and his family moved away two years ago. I miss him. I wonder if I'll ever see Jediah again."

Travel Guide
to the Past

- Zachariah and Elizabeth's baby, John, is known in the Gospels as John the Baptist. He grew up to be the prophet who lived in the Judean wilderness and preached about the Messiah. This is the John who, when he was thirty years old, baptized Jesus at the River Jordan. Many of John's followers eventually became disciples of Jesus.

- In this story, Isaac and Jediah refer to each other as "cousins," but the people living in Israel during New Testament times did not have a word specifically for "cousin." They used terms such as "kinsman" or "relative." One word they used when speaking about a male relative was "aha" which means "brother," but they frequently also used this same word when speaking of any male relative.

ZIPPORI
CITY of
PEACE

ZIPPORI

NAZARETH

MOUNT GILBOA

JERICHO

WAY
OF
BLOOD

JERUSALEM

EIN KEREM

BETHLEHEM

9. ZIPPORI

ISAAC'S COUSIN, JEDIAH, WAS WITH HIS FATHER at work in Zippori the day the Roman soldiers had come. Jediah often helped Father at home when things needed fixing but now that he was almost twelve, he was old enough to begin learning the carpentry trade.

Father was in the middle of showing Jediah how to measure and cut a large beam when Roman soldiers rode into town. All work stopped as the Romans called everyone to gather for their official announcement: All of Jediah's people, the Jews, must travel to their city of birth to register and pay taxes. Now as the soldiers galloped away, the sound of their clanking armor was replaced by an outburst of angry shouts from workers and villagers.

Jediah's father, Levi, fingered the Roman coin in his hand which read, "Zippori, the City of Peace" and shook his head with irritation.

Today was far from peaceful in this little corner of the Roman Empire. The bustling city, perched high on a hill in Galilee, was in an uproar over the latest decree from Rome. The Emperor ordered every man to go back to the city where he was born, to be counted. It wasn't easy for Jediah's father to find carpentry work, but right now he had a good job; there were many new building projects in their city, Zippori. This decree came during the busiest time and would force him to stop work in order to travel ninety miles to the city of his birth, Bethlehem.

Jediah and his father left work after the soldiers' announcement. On the way home, Father muttered, "Another census — so they can tax us for more money. How can they expect us to stop working and travel for weeks to Bethlehem and back again?"

He turned to Jediah, "What upsets me the most is that this census is their way of forcing us to belong to Rome." He paused for a minute and then started in again. "We are Jews. We belong to Yahweh…We should have our own kingdom again." Then he said in a lowered voice, "Oh, when will the Messiah come?"

Jediah was excited at the thought of traveling to Bethlehem, but he saw the agitated look on Father's face and stayed quiet.

Father set a brisk pace, so it didn't take them very long to walk home from work that day. They stopped at the water basin, outside the house, to wash up. Jediah splashed his face and curly black hair with cool water and felt it trickle down his chin and neck. His five year old sister, Eliana, came running up to them, chattering about her day.

His mother knew right away something was wrong when she saw the look on Father's face and tried to keep Eliana from pestering him.

"Hush, Eliana. Let your father sit down."

Eliana always brought a smile to Father's face. He tenderly lifted her onto his knee and gently cupped her cheeks with his large, rough hands. "I want to hear all about it," he said softly.

Eliana finished telling her little story and skipped out to the courtyard.

"Do you want to tell me what is going on?" asked Jediah's mother.

Father scratched his beard and stared blankly for a while before speaking. "Arella, today there was yet another reminder that we are forced to obey the Romans. Caesar Augustus wants a census taken to count everyone. Now we have to pack up and travel to Bethlehem." Father sighed deeply and rubbed his forehead.

Jediah's mother put her arm around his broad shoulders. "Shalom, Levi. Our lives are in the hands of the Lord. This latest order from Rome may be difficult, but we'll be all right."

During the next few days they planned and packed, baked and bartered until all was ready to begin the long journey to Bethlehem. Jediah's family would join other people from the area going that same direction — traveling in large numbers was always safer. They would head east to the Jordan River, follow it south to Jericho, and on to Jerusalem. From Jerusalem it wouldn't be far until they reached their destination; Bethlehem.

Father told Jediah, "It will take us about five days to get to Bethlehem."

Out of habit, Jediah added, "If all goes well and the donkey's fed."

Father's face softened and he put an arm around Jediah. "Yes. It will take five days to get there if all goes well." He patted Jediah's shoulder and repeated with a sigh, "If all goes well and the donkey's fed."

Jediah felt sad for his mother and father, but he had a growing sense of excitement about the journey: seeing new places, meeting new people...

Suddenly Eliana burst into the room where Jediah was packing, interrupting him with many questions. "Why are we going to Bethlehem?"

"Because father was born there, and it's easier for the Romans to count people if they all go back to where they were born."

"Is everyone in Zippori going to Bethlehem?"

"No-ooh. Not everyone was born in the city of Bethlehem. They'll go back to where they were born."

"Will Uncle Avner bring his family to Bethlehem, too? Will we see Isaac?"

Jediah's jaw dropped. He wondered why he hadn't thought of it before. "Of course — Avner would have to register at Bethlehem, just like Father. If Isaac traveled with his father, I'd get to see him again!"

Eliana tugged at Jediah's sleeve, "Will we travel by camel?"

Jediah rolled his eyes, "No. Walking is good enough for us."

Eliana was about to ask something else, but Jediah was bothered by her many questions and began walking away.

"When will we be leaving?" she yelled after him.

"Soon." He yelled back.

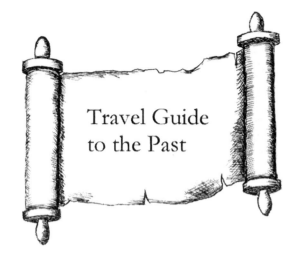

Travel Guide to the Past

• Zippori or Sepphoris (in Greek) was the capitol city of Galilee. The name, "Zippori" is the Hebrew word meaning "perched like a bird"—a good name for Jediah's city because it was perched, on top of a nine hundred foot hill. The city with its many houses glistened in the sun like a gem which could be seen for miles and miles. When Jesus gave the Sermon on the Mount and spoke about "the city on a hill that cannot be hidden," he was possibly talking about Zippori. Matthew 5:4

• The view from Jediah's hometown, Zippori, would have looked out over Nazareth, which was only four miles south, an hour's walk away. Since Zippori was an important center for trade and markets, many people from the surrounding smaller villages went there to shop and work.

10. Mount Gilboa

THE SUN HAD REACHED ITS PEAK AND JEDIAH was hot; his mouth felt as dry as the dusty road. Traveling was not as exciting as Jediah had thought it would be. They had been walking for six uneventful hours, along the flat and monotonous road below the foothills of Mount Gilboa.

Jediah had heard other people in the caravan talk about a fresh spring just off the road ahead. Now, all he could think about were his sore feet and how good the cool spring would feel, but he knew Father wanted to reach the Jordan River by nightfall and wouldn't want to stop now. He was trying to come up with a way to somehow get to the spring when he saw Eliana veer off the road ahead of them.

Jediah watched her skip along and realized she was headed toward the spring! His mind was racing; he had to quickly think of an excuse to get there too. Just then he had an idea.

"Father, Eliana left the road. I think I'd better go find her."

Father stopped and looked surprised. "Jediah, did you just ask to go take care of your sister? You've always said you didn't like following after her."

Jediah's face turned red. He looked away hoping his father didn't see through him and suspect his plan.

Father patted him on the shoulder, "Go on then. We don't want to lose Eliana."

Jediah took off. He caught up to her as she was picking a few purple irises that were growing wild. The stream was ahead of them at the bottom of a great hill.

He called after her, "Eliana, don't wander off. Let's go over to the water for a little while."

They sat down by the stream. Jediah leaned back in the thick, green grass listening to Eliana giggle as the cool, bubbling water tickled her toes. He was satisfied; his plan had worked.

"We'd better not stay much longer, Eliana. We don't want to fall too far behind."

Eliana grabbed the handful of flowers for Mother and they headed across the field for the road. Eliana noticed it first as they came around the bend, something strange whirling down the side of the hill.

"Jediah, look at that dust!" shouted Eliana.

At first, Jediah thought it was a boulder rolling through the bushes but as it neared, they noticed patches of color and heard little yips and whimpers. Jediah squinted to see what it was and realized that it was a person. It was a boy, now lying in a heap at the bottom of the hill. They ran over to him, and Jediah knelt down by the boy, wondering how badly he had been injured.

"Eliana! Run. Get help," he yelled after her. Jediah took a closer look at the boy and noticed a sling and leather pouch attached to his belt. He figured the boy must be a shepherd.

Jediah heard a voice calling out from the top of the hill, "Silas! Silas! Where are you?"

He looked up to see another boy in shepherd's clothes, holding a staff in one hand. Jediah cupped his hands around his mouth and yelled back, "I think this may be him down here!"

Hearing that, the other boy scrambled down the hill like a mountain goat; he was a fast runner. His face paled as he looked at the still body of the boy on the ground before them. He fell to his knees and asked, "Is he dead?"

"I don't think so; he's breathing. He looks pretty bruised up though. Do you know him?"

"His name is Silas. I'm his older brother, Caleb. We were tending the sheep up on top of the hill when Silas disappeared."

Caleb stayed by Silas' side, gently stroking his shoulder as Silas started to stir. Jediah noticed how deeply Caleb cared for his younger brother. When Caleb whispered something to Silas and tousled his hair, they both started laughing. Caleb helped Silas sit up and brush off the dirt.

Just then Eliana came running back with Mother and Father. They rushed over to Silas and saw he was all right except for a swollen ankle which was already showing a dark bruise.

Father told him, "You're a very lucky young man. Your only real injury is a sprained ankle. You're even luckier to have a brother who takes care of you and can make you laugh even when you're hurt."

Caleb spoke to Silas, "Now that I know you're all right, tell me how this happened. How did you end up falling down the hill? One minute you were there, and the next you had vanished."

Silas shrugged his shoulders. "I heard voices and I just wanted to get a better look at who was down here. I guess I leaned a little too far over the edge and all of a sudden I was rolling down the hill."

Caleb leaned his forehead onto Silas' and said, "You've forgotten again; you don't have wings. Next time look before you leap."

Everyone began laughing. Father offered his hand to Silas and helped him up. Caleb gave him a staff to lean on, but Silas winced in pain as he tried to stand on his sore foot. He looked at Caleb. "I can't even stand on it. How are we going to get home? How will we take care of our sheep?"

Caleb wrapped his arm around his brother. "Don't worry. I'll figure something out."

Travel Guide
to the Past

- Mount Gilboa, from the Hebrew word, gal-ba`ah, means "swollen heap." It is not a single mountain, but a series of tall hills rising to a high point of 1,700 feet.
- The stream at its base, where Jediah and Eliana soaked their feet, was the Spring of Harod. This was where the Israelite commander, Gideon selected his 300 warriors to battle the Midianites. (Judges 7:5-7)
- Jediah and his family were about seven miles west of the Jordan River when they met up with the shepherd boys, Silas and Caleb.

11. THE SHEPHERD'S CAMP

FATHER GENTLY SCOOPED UP SILAS, the injured shepherd boy. Jediah looked with admiration at Father. He always seemed to do the right thing. Silas' brother, Caleb, led the way around Mount Gilboa to their home.

Just as the whole family came around another bend, Eliana ran ahead of everyone and squealed, "I see something! Is that them?"

Jediah hurried forward to look. He had never been to a shepherds' camp before and wondered what to expect.

Caleb pointed to a cluster of large boxy, brown tents, "That's our camp!"

Jediah shaded his eyes from the late afternoon sun to stare at the circle of tents that almost blended into the shadow of the hills. He noticed a huddle of goats munching on tufts of grass around the tents and a wispy trail of smoke curling high above the camp.

Caleb turned to his little brother, being carried in Father's arms, "We're almost home. Look! I can see Mother, going into a tent."

They continued down the winding path into camp. A few women wearing dark dresses decorated with silver coins sat on mats grinding grain. A large blackened pot hung low over a glowing fire. As he walked by, Jediah took a deep breath to catch a waft of the steamy broth. The spicy aroma of lamb and onions reminded him he had nothing to eat since that morning. He felt his mouth begin to water.

Caleb led them to a large tent decorated with green tassels and called, "Mother!"

The tent flap flew open and his mother rushed out. "Caleb! I thought you were with the flock." She saw Silas being carried in Father's arms and asked, "What happened?"

Caleb told her the whole story about Silas' fall, while she spread out a soft, woven blanket for Father to set Silas down upon.

Laughing children came running up to Caleb and stared shyly at the strangers he brought into camp. Before long, men gathered around and loudly discussed Silas' fall down Mount Gilboa.

A sudden hush came over the crowd as they parted to make way for a sturdy middle aged man with a confident stride. As he reached to embrace the boys, his long, flowing robes wrapped around them. His boys were home.

The man stood up straight and tall. He thumped a fist on his large chest, "I am Amir. And you are welcome in my camp. I thank you because you've brought my sons safely home."

With that, he bowed and added, "I am indebted to you and your family. And now that it is nearing the end of the day, you must be our guests for the evening. My family has been known throughout generations for its hospitality, and you will honor us by sharing our evening meal and staying as our guests for the night."

Amir turned and pressed his hands squarely on Caleb's shoulders. He spoke with an undertone of tenderness. "I know you have been through a lot today, but our sheep still need someone to stay with them for the night. We cannot leave Baji to take care of the sheep alone. Perhaps you can bring your new friend along to help if it's all right with his father."

Jediah looked at Father who nodded his approval. The boys quickly ate a bowl of stew and took off together over the hills and open fields to where Caleb had left the sheep grazing.

Jediah asked, "Who's Baji? Is he another one of your brothers?"

Caleb laughed, "Baji is our donkey. He thinks he's part of the flock and would do anything to guard the sheep. Come on. You have to keep up. We must get to the sheep before dusk when they need our protection the most."

They returned on the path they had taken earlier in the day. Caleb knew the way well and hurried along until they climbed to the peak of the last hill. Suddenly he stopped and cupped a hand around his ear to listen.

Jediah asked, "What's wrong?"

"Come on!" Caleb shouted as he took off.

As they were running, Jediah heard the donkey braying and as they came around the bend he saw Baji stomping and kicking. In the failing light, Jediah spotted a small pack of wild jackals circling the flock.

"Yip, yip, how-ooh!" they howled. Their eerie, hollow cries sent a rush of fear through Jediah. Caleb took out his sling and picked up a few stones. He raised his arm, swinging the leather strap in fast circles, took aim, and flung a stone at the largest jackal. It hit him in the hind quarters. The jackal put its tail down and yelped in pain as he and the rest scattered into the trees.

"Hurry, Jediah. We have to gather the flock and lead them into the sheepfold."

Caleb pointed to a shallow cave in the side of a nearby hill. A low stone wall, topped with thorn bushes surrounded it, fencing it in like a pen. Caleb moved closer to his sheep, and spoke to them in a soothing voice. The sheep calmed down and trotted after him to the safety of the sheepfold. Baji, the donkey, trailed behind.

Heart pounding, Jediah looked at the edge of the field to see where the jackals had moved. He spotted one of the lambs wandering off, heading in the direction of the wild pack. The jackals grew quiet, crouched in the tall grass, waiting for the lamb to stray closer. The lamb took a few steps towards the jackals but sensed danger and stood still, unsure of which way to run.

Jediah called to the lamb, "Here, lamb. Come on." He clucked his tongue and tapped his leg, but it wasn't working. He glanced over his shoulder to see if Caleb could help, but he was busy gathering the rest of the flock. Jediah knew he had to take care of it himself before the lamb moved close enough for the jackals to pounce. He sprang forward, quickly snatching up the lamb in a tight hug, and raced back. He thought for sure he heard a growl, imagining a wild jackal charging after him, but was too scared to look back. It wasn't until he reached the safety of the sheepfold cave that he turned around and saw shining eyes still lingering at the far end of the field.

Caleb took the lamb from Jediah. "Thanks! I was looking for this little lamb. She makes thirty-seven. They're all here." He patted Jediah on the back, "That was done like a true shepherd — like King David when he was a shepherd boy."

Jediah looked at the opening of the sheep-fold wall and asked, "There's no gate. What's to keep the sheep in and the jackals out?"

Caleb squared his shoulders, "Well, I'm the gate. A shepherd, if he's a good one, lies down across the opening. Any jackal that wants my sheep will have to come past me first."

Jediah's eyes widened. "Oh…You mean you'd fight off a wild animal all alone?"

"Well, usually Silas helps me, but tonight I'm counting on you." Caleb handed him the leather sling and a few stones. Use this if you see anything coming toward us."

The boys lit a small fire near the wall. Its light and warmth brought a small measure of reassurance to them. They took turns staying up, keeping watch and tending the fire, while the other one slept.

As the flock grew restless Caleb spoke gently, "Shalom, my little sheep, I'm here to protect you."

Sometimes he stood in the middle of the flock and sang soothing melodies to quiet them. Once they calmed down, Caleb always returned to lie down across the open entrance.

Meanwhile, the wild jackals paced back and forth at the far edge of the field staring with shining eyes at the boys.

Travel Guide to the Past

• Caleb's family used Baji the donkey to guard the sheep. Donkeys will bray and bite or kick to chase away predators. A jackal is about the size of a large fox.

• Shepherds, like Caleb, kept their flocks in a protected area with a single entrance for the night. The shepherd kept guard by lying down across the opening to keep the sheep from straying and to keep wild animals or bandits from entering the pen. The shepherd's own body became the "sheep gate." Jesus uses this imagery of the Good Shepherd who lays down his life for his sheep and becomes the gate. John 10:9-11,

• The shepherd's sling is a long leather strap with a wide surface to hold a stone. As the shepherd swings the sling in a circle, he lets the stone fly out at to drive off wild animals and to guide the flock by carefully casting a stone on this side or that to direct the sheep where he wishes.

12. THE SHEPHERDS' FIELD

THE SUN WAS JUST BEGINNING TO RISE over Mount Gilboa when Jediah opened his eyes. The jackals were gone back to their dens for the day. Jediah stumbled onto his feet and watched Caleb check each sheep as he let them out of the sheepfold. "They're all here, safe and sound."

Jediah asked, "How can you tell them apart?"

Caleb smiled, "Because I'm a good shepherd. I know each of my sheep by name."

He began pointing out sheep and telling Jediah, "There's Asher, and Nisson, and Mayla, and..."

"What about that one over there?" asked Jediah pointing to a brown and white speckled ewe standing apart from the main flock.

"That's Reena, my favorite ewe. It looks like she's finally going to have her baby. See? She's pawing the ground to make a place to have her lamb."

Jediah started to run toward Reena, but Caleb held him back.

"If we rush over there now, we might startle her. Reena knows what to do. She's had many lambs."

The boys watched from a short distance until the lamb was born. Reena bleated as she licked and nudged her newborn lamb.

"Something's wrong. The little lamb should be moving by now," Caleb said as he hurried over. The lamb wasn't breathing. He rubbed the lamb's black curly coat with his cloak, trying to revive it.

Jediah pleaded, "Come on, little lamb. Breathe."

All of a sudden, the lamb sneezed and let out a long bleat. The boys watched it struggle to stand up, shake its long floppy ears and begin to nurse.

Caleb patted Jediah on the back, "Well, my friend, she's going to be all right now. What should we call her? I'd like you to pick the name."

Jediah thought a moment and said, "How about Eliana after my little sister?"

Caleb nodded. "Eliana — that's a good name."

When it was mid morning, it was time to bring the flock back to the shepherds' camp. Jediah carried the newborn lamb wrapped inside his cloak to keep it warm. Reena followed Jediah closely. From time to time she nudged his leg with

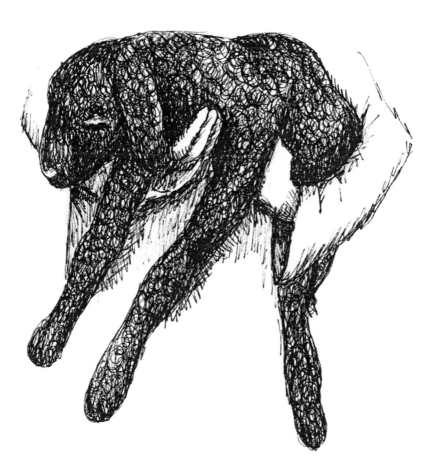

her head to remind him he was carrying her baby. This amused Jediah and he knelt down long enough for Reena to give her lamb a quick lick on its pink nose.

Jediah's father met them in the field just outside of camp. Jediah showed him the newborn lamb and told him about the jackals. Father's eyes gleamed with pride as Jediah explained how they had gathered the sheep into the sheepfold.

Jediah leaned closer to Father and whispered, "I even rescued a lamb that was wandering toward the jackals."

"We stayed up all night to keep the fire burning. Caleb lay across the opening and said, 'If they want my sheep, they'll have to come past me first!'" Both boys started laughing remembering how scared they had been.

After Father went back to the tent, Caleb went back to tend the flock, and Jediah sat down by a large tree. He picked up a blade of grass and chewed the end of it as he thought some more about his night as a shepherd. It was something he would never forget. Last night had changed him. He had never had an experience like that before.

He watched Caleb leading the sheep into a far pasture. "And to think that Caleb does this every day…We're the same age and yet Caleb seems so much older than me sometimes." Jediah recalled how bravely Caleb had defended his sheep. "I wish I had something to defend and look after."

Jediah's thoughts were interrupted by a tug on his cloak. There stood Eliana; her eyes were red and puffy and her voice was choked with tears.

"Where's Father and Mother? I can't find them. Did everyone leave? Who will take care of us?" she sobbed and sniffled.

Jediah smoothed a few strands of hair out of her eyes. "Slow down. Take a deep breath.

Father hasn't left and the shepherds have become our friends — and besides, you don't need to be afraid. I'm right here to protect you."

As the words came out of his mouth, he saw Eliana in a new way and was filled with a sense of protectiveness as her big brother. Jediah realized he cherished his little sister and admitted to himself, "She's pretty cute."

He took her hand and brought her to the tent where their parents were packing to leave. Father was bundling some of their things in his cloak. His cloak had many uses: he would spread it out for guests to sit on in their home, he used it to sleep on, or as a cover; and now he had used it to carry their belongings. Although Father valued this cloak, it was old and threadbare. Today as he pulled the corners together, the cloak shredded and tore beyond repair. Father was angry.

Jediah gasped, and Mother flicked her hand for the children to leave the tent. Jediah carefully closed the tent flaps leaving his parents to discuss what they would do now. As he spun around, he was startled to see Caleb's mother.

"Hello Jediah! I was just coming to say goodbye to you and your parents. Are they in the tent?"

"I wouldn't go in there now," he told her. "Father's cloak just tore."

" I'm sorry to hear that. What will he do?"

"I don't know. Father has no other cloak."

She winked. "I'll go see what I can find. Maybe Amir has one he can spare."

She briskly walked away and slipped into her tent. Jediah and Eliana sat down to wait. In a short while, she and Amir came back.

"Levi." Amir's deep voice resonated.

Jediah's parents looked weary and worn as they ducked out of the tent.

"I hear you are in need of a cloak."

Father glared at Jediah as Amir continued.

"Don't be upset with Jediah. He merely told my wife what had happened. We've been looking for a way to thank you and your family. You interrupted your journey to bring Silas safely home to us. Your fine son helped bring our flock to safety last night. Indeed, you have our greatest respect. We thank you and give you this cloak as a sign of our friendship."

Amir held out a beautiful cloak woven with brown fibers. "My wife had just finished weaving this from our finest wool."

Jediah looked at the long fibers interwoven more tightly than he had ever seen.

"This cloak will protect you from wind and rain better than any other. My wife is a superior weaver."

Father graciously accepted the exquisite cloak. He reached forward and embraced Amir. "I don't deserve such a gift."

Amir and his wife smiled proudly. Soon, Jediah's family said good bye and took off into the open fields toward the River Jordan. As they passed Mount Gilboa, the whole family chuckled and talked about the adventure that began with Silas rolling down the hill.

Father told Jediah, "Caleb reminded me of your cousin, Isaac."

Mother agreed. "Yes, I saw a few resemblances between Caleb and Isaac too. I miss him and the rest of the family. It's been so long since we've seen them."

Hearing Isaac's name mentioned made Jediah hope all the harder that they would meet up with Isaac and his father in Bethlehem.

Travel Guide to the Past

• Caleb's family had Karakul sheep, the oldest known breed. They are born with curly black coats that turn to browns, grays, or reddish browns as the sheep get older. They have long ears and the males grow curved horns. Karakul ewes, like Rina, are attentive mothers who keep a careful watch over their lambs. Because the mother ewes take such good care of their babies, their lambs have a better chance of surviving.

• Their long coats were sheared in the spring. Caleb's mother used sheep wool to weave clothing such as tunics and cloaks. She used goat hair to make a sturdy fabric for constructing their tents.

13. THE ROAD TO RIVER JORDAN

JEDIAH SNEEZED, "AH-AH-CHO! A-AH-CHO!" as dust blew around him and the stench of camels stuck in his nose. They were at the end of a large caravan, heading toward the River Jordan. The heavily laden camels and donkeys in front of them stirred up a haze of dust.

Jediah grumbled, "Why do we have to stay at the end of the caravan?"

Father waved his arm to gather up the family, "Come on. If we all walk faster, we can get to the front of the caravan and pass this dust storm."

He picked up Eliana, who was trying to keep up, but it had been a long day and they were all getting tired. The family began walking as quickly as they could. As they passed the merchants to the front of the line, someone called out, "Levi!"

Jediah looked around at the other travelers, wondering who called out Father's name.

Father shouted back, "Joseph! Well, well. Good to see a familiar face. Come join us."

Jediah was pretty sure he was a carpenter from Nazareth who worked with Father. Joseph made his way through the crowd, guiding a donkey carrying a pregnant young woman.

"This is my wife, Mary," Joseph said as they came closer.

"Naim Me'od, it's a pleasure to meet you, Mary. Your husband, Joseph, and I have worked together many times. He's such a humble man — I bet you don't know how good he really is at woodworking."

Mary looked at Joseph with fondness.

Father nudged Joseph with his elbow and smirked, "Don't get any ideas that you're as good as I am — yet, but you're…"

Mother stepped between the two men with one hand on her hip. "Levi," she playfully scolded and shook her head. "Someone needs to tell him what you really say when you get home from work." Mother dropped her voice and repeated what Jediah had often heard Father say, "That Joseph is the best craftsman I've seen in years. He's even better than I was at his age."

Father threw his head back and laughed. "Arella speaks the truth."

He looked at Mary, "Joseph has a reputation as a hard worker. He'll be a good provider for you and your new little one, too."

Father patted Joseph on the shoulder, "My friend, you didn't tell me you were going to be a father. Mazel Tov! Congratulations."

Mother spoke up, "Mary, you may not remember me, but I know your mother, Anna. I used to see her often at the market in Zippori. She must be very excited about a grandchild. How long after you return home will you have the baby?"

Mary replied, "We will not make it home for the baby's birth. We'll have the baby on this journey, while we're in Bethlehem." Mary looked at Joseph and smiled.

Mother said, "I can imagine that it's hard for your mother to miss the baby's birth."

"My mother was very disappointed and worried about me, but Joseph has family who live in Bethlehem. She's hoping to join us there after the baby is born."

Eliana piped up, "Bethlehem! We're on our way to Bethlehem too. Father was born in Bethlehem."

Father patted her on the head. "Yes. Although Joseph and I are not close relatives, we share the same ancestry from long ago. He and I are both from the House of David."

The two families continued on together. The air seemed cooler as they followed the route along the River Jordan. The road was edged with thick, tangled bushes and shaded by drooping branches of willow trees. It narrowed and became busier as it came to a large inn. Everyone who traveled this route planned to spend the night at this caravansary, the only one around. They entered a bustling courtyard enclosed on all four sides by tall brick walls. Jediah spotted a fountain in the center. He was just about to run toward it when he heard Father.

"It's already getting dark. We need to stay close together and find the innkeeper."

They made their way past a group of bellowing camels tethered in the courtyard, and came to the main building. Joseph and Father stepped forward to knock on the door. As they waited, they heard people talking inside the inn, but no one came to the door.

Father looked at Joseph with a puzzled face and then pounded the door with his fist as hard as he could. The conversation inside stopped. A few seconds later the door burst open sending a ray of sudden brightness into the dark courtyard. Jediah squinted to see the man who opened the door. He had a gruff appearance: small beady eyes, a patchy beard, and disheveled hair.

"Whaddya want?" he snarled with his mouth full of food.

"Well sir, we need a room for the night," replied Joseph.

"Not here. The place is full."

Joseph appealed to the man, "Excuse me, but my wife is pregnant and cannot go on any farther today. Surely there's somewhere…"

"Didn't ya hear me?" the innkeeper barked. "You'll have to look somewhere else."

Jediah's father stepped forward, "Please, we have children and there's no where else to stay for miles! We would even stay in a shed, or…"

"No! Now you've disturbed my meal for long enough!" The heavy beamed door made a deep boom as he slammed it shut in front of them.

The weary travelers felt a deepening gloom as they stood in the dark courtyard. Eliana whimpered and tugged at Mother's cloak. "He's a mean man. I wouldn't want to stay here..." She rubbed her eyes with her fists, "but I'm tired. Where will we sleep?"

Joseph spoke next. "If only we were already in Bethlehem; we'd be warmly welcomed by relatives, not left standing outside still looking for a place to sleep."

Mother usually had a pleasant temperament, but the frustration of being turned away in such a rude manner provoked her. She spoke with pointed words, "Yes. We will be in Bethlehem soon, but tonight we have tired children and not many options. What are we going to do, Levi?"

Father clenched his jaw and silently stared at the starless sky. Jediah could tell by the way he was tugging at his beard he was annoyed. A cool breeze picked up and Jediah pulled his cloak up around his ears. When a bolt of lightning flashed on the horizon, followed by the rumbling threat of a distant storm, everyone knew it would be raining before long.

Mary, gently spoke. "Shalom." She added, in a voice barely over a whisper, "We should trust the Lord. He will surely help us."

Jediah didn't say anything but it seemed certain they would be sleeping outside tonight in the cold rain.

Travel Guide to the Past

- Jediah's father and Joseph were both "tekton" which is a Hebrew word used to describe a builder or someone who works with wood or stone. It demanded a great deal of physical strength as well as skill.

- The large inn where Jediah's family first tried to stay was called a "caravansary." It was a tall rectangular building with various open room areas for travelers. The animals were kept in the courtyard. Sleeping at the caravansary could be very loud, especially when large caravans of camels stayed overnight.

- Naim Me'od is a Hebrew phrase that means, "It's a pleasure to meet you."

14. THE CAMPFIRE

A DARK SHADOW FELL ACROSS THE EDGE of the caravansary courtyard. A hushed voice from someone lurking in the darkness caught their attention, "Psst — over here!"

"Who's there?" Joseph called out as he took a few uncertain steps toward the voice.

"Over here, behind the inn," the voice insisted.

Jediah stood still, frozen in place as Father and Joseph followed the voice around the corner and disappeared from view. A few moments later, Joseph popped his head out and motioned for everyone to follow.

As they came closer, Jediah saw the mysterious person was an older woman. Her shoulders were rounded forward and her second chin wiggled as she talked. "Follow me. I know a place you can stay for the night." She motioned for them to follow her up a grassy slope.

Mary held onto Joseph's arm as they began up the path; their donkey following. At the top, they came to a small shed near the edge of a field. It was made of mud bricks with a thatched roof. Jediah figured that it was smaller than their house but large enough for all of them to sleep in for the night. Their guide set about lighting a lantern and motioned for them to go in.

"My name is Hannah. I overheard my husband turn you away. This is our storage shed for extra bed rolls and other supplies. I often bring people here when there's no room in the inn. It's a little run down but it will be dry. There's a storm brewing, you know."

Father spoke, "We can all breathe a sigh of relief. Thank you for this shelter."

Hannah bobbed her head up and down. "I'm always glad to help. Now I have to hurry back to the inn. I'll check on you folks a little later."

Jediah stepped outside and saw that the storm was still in the distance so he quickly gathered a few pieces of wood to start a small fire. Soon Mother, Father and Joseph joined him. Eliana was already asleep in the shelter where Mary was also resting for the night. As they sat outside by the fire, its warmth melted tensions and soothed their frazzled tempers.

"Well" said Joseph, "The Lord surely provides in surprising ways, doesn't he?"

They all agreed with Joseph and soon fell into friendly conversation.

Mother asked, "Joseph, have you and Mary thought of a name for your baby?"

"We've decided to call him Yeshua, Jesus."

"Oh, Yeshua, the Lord saves. It's such a beautiful name; so full of hope. How did you come to choose that name?"

Joseph shifted uncomfortably. He picked up a small stone and distractedly rolled it in his palm as he said slowly, "Well, Arella, it's a complicated story. Let's just say Mary had an inspiration for the name."

"Well, I think it's a lovely thought. We can all stand a little more inspiration, especially now-a-days when things look so bleak with the Romans overtaking our land." Mother sighed deeply and continued. "Oh, yes, when it comes to the Messiah, we all need inspiration and patience. The Messiah; the hero promised by our prophets — the One who will free us for good from the Romans."

"If only we didn't have to wait so long!" Father grumbled. He poked a stick into the fire causing sparks to crackle and jump. "It's already been hundreds of years."

"Levi, we can't give up hoping," Mother said firmly. "He may come at any time, perhaps soon. We need to expect the impossible."

With growing enthusiasm, she turned to Joseph, "You and Mary are having a baby in Bethlehem — perhaps even your child could be the Promised One! They say the Messiah will be born in Bethlehem from the line of David."

Then Jediah got caught up in her excitement. "What about Galilee? They also said he would come from Galilee."

Once Jediah's words were spoken, they seemed to hang in the air. Everyone became silent, remembering that Joseph and Mary were from Nazareth in Galilee and would be returning there with the baby. They all looked at Joseph as they realized that all of the prophecies about the Messiah's birth seemed to fit Mary and Joseph.

Joseph's face flushed. He quickly looked away from them, down at the fire. After a long pause he said, "You're right, Arella. Everything you said is true. Now is the time to wait with more hope than ever." He shrugged as he got up from the fire, "Excuse me now. I'm going to check on Mary."

Mother turned to Father and whispered, "Like I said, we need to have hope but could it be Joseph and Mary?"

Father raised his eyebrows. "Everything you said made sense, but Joseph and Mary are poor, ordinary people. I always had imagined the Messiah's birth would be grand, something fit for a king, not taking place on a journey."

Their discussion ended abruptly as Hannah came back to join them at the fire. "I thought you folks must be hungry." She opened a cloth full of sweet dates, slabs of cheese and freshly baked pita. She smiled at Jediah and handed him a juicy pomegranate.

"Barak and I have had a long day at the inn. He was tired by the time you folks showed up. I'm sorry he turned you away so rudely. We don't have enough rooms for all the travelers coming through for the census."

Hannah sighed, allowing herself a moment to relax. "Well, now tell me. Where are you headed?"

Father answered, "We're on our way to the town of Bethlehem."

As Joseph came back from the shelter to join them, he added, "We're planning to travel on through Jericho."

Hannah's face lit up. "Jericho. My sister and her husband run an inn at Jericho. Go to the Dafna Inn and mention that Hannah sent you. She'll find a place for you to stay. If you leave at sunup you should be there by early afternoon, before the busy time."

Mother held Hannah's hand, "Thank you for your hospitality. You've been very helpful."

Hannah smiled kindly. "I'm just glad I could help you. I hope you have a safe trip. Goodnight," she said as she returned to the inn.

A crisp breeze picked up and soon a gentle rain snuffed out the fire. They settled comfortably inside the shed, sleeping soundly as the rain continued splattering on the roof.

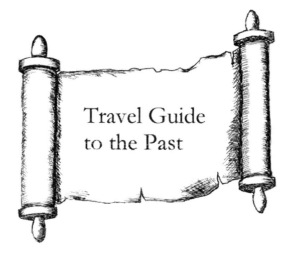

Travel Guide
to the Past

• 'Yeshua' is the Greek word for 'Jesus'.

• Levi, like most Jewish people in Palestine, was unhappy with the Roman occupation.

• Many hoped for a political Messiah to free them and believed the Messiah's coming would be soon. They knew he would come from the House of David; he would be born in Bethlehem, David's city; and he would begin his ministry in Galilee — the land Isaiah prophesied would see a great light and hear a message of great joy. Isaiah 9:1 / Matthew 4:15

• Jediah's family had about twenty miles to travel from this inn on the River Jordan to reach Jericho.

15. A Muddy Road to Jericho

The rainstorm had stopped by the time Jediah woke. He stood and stretched, looked around the room, and realized he was the last one to get up. Everyone else was already outside, talking and laughing. He could smell the aroma of fresh bread as he came out of the shelter.

"Good morning, sleepyhead," Mother chirped. "Have some bread and cheese. We're going to be leaving soon for Jericho."

Jediah began walking toward Father and heard Joseph say, "Well, Levi, it was good traveling with you yesterday but I think we're going to stay behind, and leave later today. Mary could use a little more rest, and our old donkey will have a hard time with these muddy roads. We'll leave later when the roads are dry."

Father shook Joseph's hand, "Seeing you and Mary was an unexpected pleasure. I hope we'll see you again along the way, but if not, have a safe travel."

"If we don't meet up again on this trip," Joseph replied, "please come to see us and the baby back in Nazareth."

"We'll be sure to do that," Father promised. He turned to the family and said, "Let's go. We should be in the city of Jericho by midday — if all goes well and the donkey's fed."

Jediah and Eliana laughed to hear Father use the family saying. They quickly made their way back down the hill and took the path to the main road. Joseph was right. The wet, soggy mud made walking difficult. They trudged along the road, trying to avoid slipping on the soft, squishy spots.

Eliana asked Father, "Are we almost there? Are we almost to the City of the Balms?"

Father was puzzled and not quite sure what she meant. Jediah laughed and asked her, "Where did you hear Jericho called that?"

"I heard people on the road yesterday. They called it 'Jericho, City of the Balms!'"

Father held back a laugh, "Well, you almost have it right. I think they said City of the Palms. Jericho is full of different kinds of palm trees."

Jediah thought he heard something; the galloping rhythm of hoof beats growing louder.

He looked back. There was just enough early sunlight for him to see the outline of a chariot racing towards them. Jediah yelled, "Look out! Move!"

Everyone scurried over just in time to make room for a black galloping horse pulling a Roman chariot. A blur of red and silver swooshed past them.

They watched as the chariot continued whirling farther down the road until a wheel hit the edge of the road and the whole chariot tipped with a thud in the mud. Jediah and Father exchanged looks. Father was angry.

"That Roman almost ran us over."

"Now Levi, watch your temper. He's a Roman soldier," Mother warned.

Father pointed at the soldier struggling to get up from the mud. "He doesn't look hurt," Father smirked, "but he'll need a good cleaning!"

They all chuckled at the sight of this pompous Roman soldier covered in thick, slimy muck.

Father said, "Well, Jediah, I suppose we should go see if he needs help with the chariot."

When they got there, the driver was wading deep in mud, trying to calm his high-strung horse and lead her out of the thick sludge.

"What happened?" Father asked.

"Isn't it plain to see?" barked the Roman. "She pulled the chariot too close to the edge, and the wheel got stuck, tipping the whole thing over. Chariots weren't made for these muddy Judean roads!"

The spirited horse tossed its head and blew air out of its nostrils as if in agreement.

Jediah looked at the Roman soldier. His red cape was soggy and heavy, clinging to his back, and his armor was smeared with mud. His sandals sloshed with each step.

Father spoke up first. "I'm Levi and this is my son Jediah."

The Roman replied in a tone of authority, "I'm Cassius, Commander of the Centurions." He pointed to the chariot. "You and your son grab that end and lift when I tell you. I'll take this end."

Jediah watched Father's face. No one ever gave him orders or spoke to him in that tone of voice. Father clenched his jaw and kept silent.

He knew it would be foolish and dangerous to argue with a Roman soldier.

They lifted together. With three of them, it wasn't hard to get the chariot upright, but the wheels were still stuck.

As Cassius walked over to harness his horse, Jediah noticed a clinking. He looked over to see several rows of medals mounted by ribbons on Cassius' metal breastplate. Jediah stared at them, shining in the sun; there were so many, and each one was unique.

Cassius slowly led the horse forward and told Jediah, "Push!"

Jediah leaned forward, pushing against the back of the chariot with his palms, when suddenly, the chariot loosened and pulled ahead.

"Whoa!" he hollered as his sandals slipped. Jediah fell into the muck. He was embarrassed to fall in front of the men. Cassius chuckled as he extended his had to help him up. Jediah had seen plenty of soldiers in Zippori but none of them would have lent a hand to help him. Jediah stared at this Roman commander. Deep down he knew Cassius was different.

Cassius asked, "You're headed to Jericho?"

Father nodded.

"You were smart to have left early. The city is overflowing with people coming for the chariot races at the Hippodrome. You'll be lucky to find any place to stay today."

Father told him, "We're hoping to stay at the Dafna Inn."

"Dafna? I know Dafna. She runs a nice inn. Many centurions stay there."

"Will we see you there?" Jediah asked.

"Yes. I'll be there but, in Jericho, Centurions keep to themselves." He held out a muddy hand as if to stop any further questions and said curtly, "I have to go. I have important business that won't wait for me."

Cassius stepped into the chariot and nodded to Jediah and Father. The horse snorted and stamped the ground, impatient to get going. Cassius snapped the reins. Away they raced, down the road to Jericho.

Jediah looked down at his mud caked sandals. Next to his foot, something flashed. Half hidden in a muddy footprint lay something silver. He bent over and plucked it up, carefully using a clean corner of his cloak to rub off the dirt. A medal! It was large, almost filling the palm of his hand, and had an engraving of a Roman eagle on one side, a Roman centurion on the other.

Cassius was already gone, far in the distance. Jediah wasn't sure what to do with the treasure he found. His first thought was to show Father. Together they could find Cassius in Jericho. As Jediah walked back to the rest of his family, he overheard Father talking to Mother.

"Well, he seemed nice enough out here — but Romans are not to be trusted. He said he was staying at the Dafna Inn, but to be honest, I hope we don't see him there. Who knows what he would be like in Jericho among the other soldiers."

Jediah stopped by the side of the road and secretly tucked the medal into an inner pocket. He felt a strange combination of emotions: excitement for finding the medal but shame for keeping it a secret from Father. Regardless of how he felt, Jediah decided he would find some way to return it to Cassius in Jericho — without Father knowing.

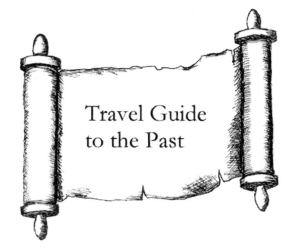

Travel Guide
to the Past

- Roman chariots were designed for racing and were made of light materials such as wood and woven leather. The chariot weighed around 100 pounds so a horse could easily pull it around the track during races.

- A Roman centurion was in charge of 100 men. The rank of these commanders was equivalent to that of a modern day colonel.

- The Roman medal Jediah found was called a phalera (fa-lair-a). It was a circular shape approximately four inches in diameter. These discs were made of precious gold, silver, or bronze. A Roman soldier was awarded a phalera for outstanding service.

- The Hippodrome Cassius mentioned was a huge stadium-like building where chariot races and horse competitions were held.

16. THE DAFNA INN

THERE WERE SO MANY LUSH PALM trees Jediah could hardly see the blue sky when he looked up. Ever since early morning they had been trudging through the nothingness of the stark and stony desert, but now they were in Jericho. The city was full of new sights and colors: green vegetation and bright flowers in well kept parks, bubbling fountains, and the flash of red and silver from hundreds of Roman soldiers rushing to and from the Hippodrome. Crowds of wealthy people, dressed in fine, colorful robes milled about the marketplace.

Jediah felt self-conscious about his mud-caked tunic, and pulled the front of his cloak together, hoping to hide it.

Eliana raised her nose and sniffed. "What's that yummy smell?"

Mother closed her eyes. "Mmm — balsam," she breathed deeply. "Jericho is known for growing the finest balsam. It brings back so many memories."

Eliana asked, "What's it for? Do you eat it?"

Mother smiled. "No. It's used for many things, but it's wonderful for babies. When you and Jediah were born, I gave you baths in balsam. It made your skin so soft and smooth."

Eliana tugged on Mother's sleeve pleading, "Can we buy some for Joseph and Mary's baby?"

Mother suggested, "Let's find the inn first. We'll have to come back to the market later to get fresh food. We can think about it then."

Jediah pressed his hand to his brow, shadowing his eyes, as he searched for Cassius among the throngs of Roman soldiers. A group of soldiers, all talking loudly about the races, bumped into Jediah as they boyishly shoved each other and laughed.

"How am I going to find him?" Jediah muttered under his breath.

"Find who? Who are you looking for?" Eliana demanded.

Jediah's stomach grew tight. He had to make her stop asking him questions that might reveal his secret about finding Cassius.

Just then, he and Eliana both overheard a soldier behind them say, "Whoa, Damien, we almost passed the Dafna Inn!"

Jediah's eyes followed the soldiers as they turned into the courtyard.

"Look! The Dafna Inn!" Eliana blurted, pointing with an outstretched arm. She turned to Mother and Father. "How do we find Dafna? How will we know what she looks like?"

A woman carrying an armload of laundry passed them as she hurried out of the inn. Father called after her, "Excuse me. Do you know Dafna?"

"Who are you?" the woman asked in a pleasant but cautious voice.

"My name is Levi. Hannah sent us here. Do you know Dafna?"

The woman's face softened into a warm smile as she walked back toward them. Although she was younger and thinner, the friendly expression on her face reminded Jediah of Hannah.

"I'm Dafna, Hannah's sister," she said. "My inn is usually full with Roman soldiers and I often have to turn travelers away, but if Hannah has sent you, I'm sure I can find a room."

While the adults talked, Jediah wandered over to the center of the courtyard to study the faces of soldiers coming in and out. They all looked the same in their uniforms. It would be much harder to find Cassius than Jediah thought.

Jediah muttered under his breath, "He must be here somewhere. He said he would be staying here, at the inn, for the night."

"Jediah!" Father yelled. "Come back. Dafna is showing us to the room."

As Jediah came toward them, Dafna looked at him and clucked her tongue. "You're the second person today who came here looking like a monkey in a mud bath. The other one was a soldier; he was madder than a wet hen."

Jediah felt embarrassed by Dafna's comments about his muddy tunic, but he perked up on hearing her mention the muddy soldier, figuring it must be Cassius! "Now" he thought, "if only she could say where Cassius could be found."

Dafna went on, "I was just heading over to do laundry when I met up with you folks. If you'd like, I could wash your boy's tunic. I have an extra that I can lend you. It used to fit one of my boys. "

Mother replied, "We'd appreciate that, Dafna. This is Jediah's only tunic, and we still have a few days of travel before I'll have a chance to wash it."

As Dafna unlocked the door she said, "Here's your room. I'll run the spare tunic back up for the boy in a minute. Let me know if you need anything else."

Father thanked her as she left. Jediah walked over to a window overlooking the court-yard and leaned out hoping to spot Cassius. "If only I could find a way to meet up with Cassius without lying to Father." He looked around hoping no one had overheard him. "I can't keep a Roman soldier's medal. I have to find a way to talk to Dafna — alone."

"Can we go back to the market now?" Eliana begged. "I want to smell that balsam again."

Father replied, "I overheard you talking to Mother about buying some for Joseph and Mary's baby. That's a very kind thought."

Eliana proudly tilted her pointed little chin and smiled at him. "So, does that mean we can go now?"

"I think we're settled in enough. Let's look around Jericho."

Before he knew it, a plan had hatched in Jediah's mind. His family would be leaving for the marketplace and he could easily think of a reason to stay behind. Here at last, was his chance to talk to Dafna without Father knowing. It seemed almost too good to be true.

"Father, I'll stay here and wait for Dafna to bring the clean tunic. I don't need to go to the market, do I?"

Jediah felt his face flush and quickly looked away from Father. This was the closest he had ever come to lying. For a moment, he considered telling Father about everything. "No," Jediah decided. "I'm going to find Cassius and return the medal on my own."

He regretted keeping the medal a secret from Father but he'd been hiding it for most of the day and couldn't tell him now. He would wait until they were gone and talk to Dafna.

Travel Guide
to the Past

• Wealthy people from Jerusalem came to Jericho because of its warm climate and lush vegetation. King Herod built a palace in this city. This is the city where the tax collector, Zacchaeus, climbed a tree in order to see Jesus above the crowds.

■Balsam trees are valued for healing qualities. Balsam is also known as the "Balm of Gilead." Its dark brown bark has a pleasant sweet and spicy fragrance. Balsam is both rare and difficult to grow.

17. Dafna's Courtyard

Jediah stood at the window watching his family leave the inn and disappear into Jericho's crowded streets. Now he was free to find Dafna and ask her about the Roman soldier, Cassius. Maybe she would know where to find him. There was a quick knock on the door and Dafna entered with the extra tunic.

Jediah began to ask, "Do you know where..." but she was in a rush and didn't hear him.

"I have to get back to the courtyard and stir the stew before it burns."

He slipped into the borrowed tunic. It was too large for him; the hem dragged on the floor, but it would do. He hurried down to the court-yard, his mind racing with the plan he had been forming. There, he saw Dafna by the fire, talking with a group of Romans.

Jediah stood over to the side waiting until she was alone before asking about Cassius. He took the medal out from his pocket to look at it one last time, and rubbed it with his oversized tunic; then, fascinated by its shine, he gently turned it back and forth in his palm to dance the sunlight off it.

"Hey. That's shining right in my eyes," shouted one of the soldiers. He had an angry face with a wide mouth and a jagged scar on his sweaty cheek.

"Oh, I'm sorry." Jediah said as he quickly shoved the medal back into his pocket. He didn't want to upset a Roman soldier.

"Hey," the irritated soldier snapped. "What is that? What did you hide in your pocket? Let me see."

Dafna stood up and spoke to the angry soldier. "What's going on, Flavius?"

He held up his hand and warned her, "Stay out of this, Dafna."

Jediah quickly apologized again. "I'm sorry. I didn't mean to flash it in your…"

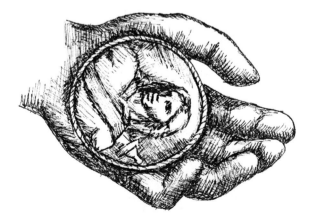

Flavius interrupted. "I said, 'Let me see it!'"

The Roman pushed Jediah backward and he stepped on the hem of the oversized tunic, stumbling to the ground. The soldier reached down, grabbing the medal from Jediah's pocket. His pale eyes narrowed as he examined the medal.

"Where did you get this?" he snarled.

The other soldiers stepped in to see what the commotion was about.

"Well, well," gloated Flavius, while holding the medal with outstretched arm. "It looks like we caught a thief red-handed. The only way to get a soldier's medal is to kill him or steal it." He paused for a sarcastic laugh. "And I am certain a scrawny boy like you didn't kill a Roman soldier!"

Jediah spluttered, "I — no — wait…"

Flavius bent down into Jediah's face threatening, "Do you know what we do to boys who steal from Roman soldiers?"

A deep, gruff voice from behind them demanded, "Flavius, why do you have my medal? I've been looking for it all day." It was Cassius.

Flavius pointed his sword at Jediah. "This little rug-rat must have stolen it from you."

Cassius' face flushed red, the tendons in his neck tightened as he drew his sword. "Who stole it? Let me at him!"

The soldiers parted, and Cassius strode forward to see Jediah on the ground frozen in fear.

"You, boy? You stole my medal?" he said in a voice revealing disappointment and betrayal.

"No." Jediah stopped and stammered, "It's not what you think."

He heard footsteps pounding toward them and Father's voice boomed like a lion protecting its young, "Jediah, are you all right? What's going on here?"

Cassius spoke flatly, "Your son was hiding a very valuable medal of mine. I think he stole it. He was just about to explain how he got it."

Father's eyes were dark and angry. "Is this true, Jediah? Did you steal this?"

Jediah felt as though a giant hand inside his stomach grabbed onto it and wouldn't let go. He turned to Cassius and said with a trembling voice. "Earlier this morning when we helped you with the chariot, it must have fallen off. I found it on the ground as you were riding away so I picked it up and decided to try to find you here. I was just coming to ask Dafna if she knew where you were."

Cassius slid his sword back into the leather sheath. "Of course — the muddy road this morning. That makes sense. Flavius, he's telling the truth. This is the family that helped me out of the mud earlier."

Flavius laughed, "I've never seen Cassius so dirty! We thought he knew how to drive his chariot, but apparently he needs a lesson or two about mud."

Jediah got to his feet. Cassius looked him in the eye. "It seems this was a case of false impressions. I should have known you weren't the stealing type. Thank you for bringing back the medal."

As Jediah and his family walked away from the soldiers everyone was shaken except Eliana. She began telling Jediah about the market but Father put a finger to his lips.

"Not now, Eliana. I need to talk to Jediah alone. Stay with Mother."

Father put his arm around Jediah's shoulder and they went behind the inn where it was quiet. Father sat down on a pile of wood and motioned for Jediah to sit next to him.

Father sighed deeply and asked, "Why didn't you tell me about the medal?" He rubbed his forehead and continued. "Why did you keep it a secret from me?"

Jediah looked away from Father's face to avoid meeting the disappointment in his eyes. Choking back emotion, Jediah told him, "I heard you say you didn't want to see Cassius again."

"That may be true, but returning the medal to him was the right thing to do. You should know I would have helped you with that. I'm your father. I always want to help you. Please don't keep secrets from me again. Do you understand?"

"I understand, Father. I'm sorry."

Jediah leaned his head onto Father's chest and Father pressed him close. Jediah liked to think of himself as grown up, but he quietly admitted, "I thought I could handle this on my own, but I needed you."

"Jediah, we have to work together; I'm counting on you, now more than ever. Tomorrow will be the most dangerous part of our journey."

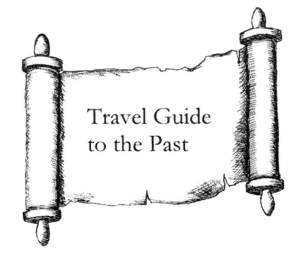

Travel Guide to the Past

- Romans imposed serious punishments when their laws were broken. Under Roman law, thieves were put to death for stealing. Jediah was fortunate that Cassius recognized him and believed that he was trying to return the medal he had found in the mud.

18. THE WAY OF BLOOD

EVERYTHING ABOUT IT LOOKED dangerous: narrow paths with corners blocking the view, and steep cliffs with tall rocks — a perfect hiding place for thieves. This was the route known as "The Way of Blood." This sun baked valley with its winding paths led from Jericho up to Jerusalem.

It had a reputation as a deadly trap for unsuspecting travelers passing through its deep canyons.

Before Jediah and his family left Dafna's Inn this morning, she introduced them to a wealthy merchant, Ezra. His spice caravan was leaving Jericho, planning to pass through the Way of Blood, and he agreed to let them travel along with his crew through this dangerous part of road. Ezra was confident and poised. His bright red turban and gold earrings made him look like a king. He assured Father that he had been through this section of road many times and was fully aware of its reputation for danger.

They were already a long distance from the lush palms and fountains of Jericho, well on their way into the harsh, dry, wasteland. They walked alongside heavily packed camels strung in a single file. Ezra continually rode up and down the long line making sure all of his men were positioned where they could be ready to protect his merchandise.

Seeing the narrow path just ahead, Father sensed this would be a likely area for an ambush. He said firmly, "Stay close, Eliana."

She clutched Father's cloak. He nervously gripped Mother's hand. "Arella, we need to move faster. I want to get us away from the back of the caravan. It's the most defenseless. We want to be as near to the front of the caravan as we can get." He led them farther ahead where they would be more secure.

As Ezra rode past them this time, he leaned down to Father and said in a hushed voice, "Beware. Thieves often hide ahead, behind those large rocks, where the path narrows. They attack stragglers at the end of the caravan. You were smart to move your wife and children forward." He paused to calm his fidgeting horse and spoke slowly to emphasize his next bit of advice. "A word to the wise: Do not stop, especially if an attack begins. You'll be safest to keep moving along with the camels. The travelers who stop find themselves in danger." Father nodded. "Thanks for the warning."

The sun was blistering hot in the narrow, rocky passageway that wound along the edges of steep ravines with overhanging rocks. Jediah wiped the sweat off his forehead with the back of his arm and looked about uneasily with a deepening sense of foreboding. He remembered he still had the sling Caleb had given him and stooped to pick up a few sharp stones to use for protection, if it came to that.

Only the noisy bellowing of the camels interrupted the eerie silence among the caravan. Everyone was on edge: looking around and listening for any sign of trouble. Jediah felt the tension mounting when suddenly a woman's shriek signaled their worst fear was upon them. A group of men, with blood curdling yelps, bolted from behind the jagged rocks. They all had daggers drawn as they ran toward the back of the caravan.

Frightened screams and panic swept over the group. Even the animals understood the fearful danger in the air. Donkeys brayed and kicked; snorting camels stamped and threw their heads. The camel handlers tapped their sticks to make the animals move along at a trot to get away from the bandits. The road finally widened and the camels ran forward, moving together in a large group.

Father shouted, "Let's get between those camels! Come on!"

He swung Eliana up onto his back and Mother held Jediah's hand as they ran into the middle of the moving herd. Jediah ran as fast as he could. He knew they had to keep hidden between the camels. It was risky. The galloping camels swung their strong legs awkwardly, stirring up a cloud of dust.

"Don't trip. Please don't trip," Jediah repeated to himself. His feet felt large and clumsy. He was afraid of falling and being trampled by the camels, left to face the bandits alone. He told himself again. "Don't fall!"

The attack lasted only a few minutes, but it seemed longer than that to Jediah. The shouts grew fainter and the camels slowed. The dust began to settle and the group came to a stop. Father looked around, tense with the uncertainty. "Be on your guard. I don't know if they're gone."

Everyone was relieved when they saw Ezra ride by and shout, "They're gone. We'll be all right now."

Six camel drivers who had been at the end of the caravan during the attack ran up to Ezra. Father and Jediah rushed over to hear what happened.

Ezra offered the camel drivers some water and asked, "Are you all right?"

At first, the men couldn't speak. They bent over, hands on their knees, trying to catch their breath.

Then one of the men spoke up, "There must have been more than a dozen hiding in the rocks! When the commotion began, I looked up and saw them run out."

Another man added in panting breaths, "They were wild men — vicious — came at us swinging knives and daggers." He paused and wiped his brow. "They came so close I could smell their hot stinking breath. I thought for sure they meant to kill us but this time they wanted riches, not blood. We did as you said, Ezra, and un-fastened the saddlebags on the last two camels, dropped them, and started running."

Ezra flashed a wide, triumphant grin. "Well done! We were ready for those thieves this time." He joined his men as they shouted in victory.

Jediah was confused. He whispered to Father, "How could Ezra be happy that his men had left his bags for the bandits to take? Shouldn't they have tried to fight the thieves? After all, it was their job to protect Ezra's merchandise."

Father shrugged his shoulders. "I don't understand either."

Jediah turned to Ezra and blurted out, "But you lost so much merchandise. How can you and your men celebrate a victory?"

Ezra explained, "Before we left Jericho we filled several saddle bags with old, broken pottery and packed a few of our cheaper merchandise on the top. We loaded those on the camels at the end of the caravan. I told my men, if any thieves came, to let them take those bags."

He grinned broadly and broke into a laugh. "Wait until they take a closer look and find nothing but garbage! This time, they got what they deserved." Ezra punched the air with his fist. "That will teach them not to steal from me!"

He and his men broke out into jubilant whoop-whoop-whoops once again.

Jediah and Father walked back to Mother and Eliana and told them about how Ezra's shrewd plan had succeeded. Father ran his fingers through his hair, damp from sweat, and said, "That was a close one. The Lord was watching out for us. Jediah, do you know the prayer I asked you to memorize before we left home?"

Jediah nodded.

"Now would be a good time to recite it."

Jediah stood straight and tall as he began in a firm voice, "The Lord is my shepherd. There is nothing I shall want...Even though I walk through the dark valley, I fear no harm for you are at my side..."

Jediah thought about how he had heard these same words declared many times at the synagogue, but they meant so much more now after he had experienced for himself the "valley of death" that King David had written about in this psalm.

After a short rest, Ezra signaled the caravan to set out again. The next leg of the road left the valley and rose in a steep climb to Jerusalem. There were no other surprises for the remainder of this part of the journey except for occasional little lizards that scurried across the trail as they came near. Jediah and his family knew the worst part was over. They made it safely out of the Way of Blood.

Travel Guide
to the Past

• Jediah's family traveled on the same treacherous pathway that Jesus later spoke about in the parable of the Good Samaritan. This route was so dangerous it was also called the "Valley of the Shadow of Death."

• The Judean desert landscape is not sandy like the Sahara Desert but made up of rugged, stark limestone cliffs and valleys. Jesus spent forty days of fasting in this deserted area before beginning his public life.

• The prayer that Jediah's family recited is from Psalm 23, the Good Shepherd Psalm.

• The route through the desert area from outside Jericho to Jerusalem is a steadily upward hike of 3,500 feet. Its twisting canyon roads cover a distance of 15 miles.

19. Gethsemane

The whole mount looked enchanted. Olive trees with gnarled trunks and shimmering leaves shaded a lush landscape sprinkled with bright pink and yellow flowers. At the base of the hill, a stone wall encircled the most beautiful garden Jediah had ever seen. As they drew closer, he heard laughter and saw people strolling along the winding pathways lined with sweet smelling jasmine. Some people sat under the peaceful shade of rose arbors, listening to singers chanting sacred psalms.

Mother turned to Father, "Levi, look! We can see Jerusalem. Could we stop here in Gethsemane and rest for a while?"

So this was the Garden of Gethsemane, thought Jediah, then that hillside teeming with trees must be the Mount of Olives. They walked along paths until they came to a shady area to sit and began talking about where they would spend the Sabbath.

Jediah watched an elderly woman tending a rosebush's delicate blooms. The woman called, "Simeon, would you bring me that spade?"

An old man with a silver beard, picked up the garden tool. Jediah figured he must be Simeon. As the man passed by, he caught Jediah's curious look and smiled.

He leaned toward Jediah, "That's my wife, Sarah. She loves gardening. She always says that she wants me to come here to keep her company." He chuckled. "But I think she brings me along just to hand her things."

Sarah began digging as Simeon shuffled back toward them. "Are you folks traveling through?"

Father answered, "Yes. We're on our way to Bethlehem for the census."

Simeon stroked his bearded chin and nodded knowingly. "Do you already have a place to stay?"

"As a matter of fact, we don't. I'm Levi. My wife, Arella, and I were just talking about that now. To be honest, we've just arrived and don't know where to begin looking. Have any suggestions?"

The wrinkles in Simeon's face creased even deeper as he smiled broadly.

"I happen to know of a comfortable, clean place..." His eyes sparkled as he said loudly, "with a cute cook."

Sarah stopped digging and playfully wagged her finger at him. "Simeon, I heard that." She stood up and brushed herself off. "Will you folks be joining us tonight then?"

Father and Mother exchanged looks.

Father answered, "Todah Rabbah. Thank you. That's very kind of you."

Jediah's family followed Simeon and Sarah to their house. It was in the center of Jerusalem, built next to the outer wall of the Temple. Father helped Sarah carry sleeping mats up to the top terrace on the flat roof. Jediah looked out from this rooftop room and was able to see into the Temple courtyards.

Sarah was showing them how to open the awning when they heard a group of people in the courtyard. She leaned over the patio railing to wave and called out, "Erev Tov! Shalom!"

Sarah turned to Jediah's family and explained, "Our three sons and their families have come for the Sabbath meal. Come down to join us after you are settled."

Soon the house was full of laughter and lively conversation. Simeon's grandsons played stringed instruments, while the men sang, and bounced the young ones on their knees.

The women in the kitchen broke into dance, twirling arm in arm, while the food cooked. When Sarah announced that dinner was ready, Jediah's eyes popped. It was a feast: roasted lamb kebabs rubbed with cumin, steaming rice with pine nuts, hummus and flat bread, stuffed grape leaves, sliced cucumbers with black olives, goat cheese, and juicy red pomegranates.

After they finished eating, Simeon opened his mouth to speak but hesitated for a short moment as he looked at Sarah, who shook her head as if to say, "Not now, Simeon."

He disregarded her warning, cleared his throat, and continued. "Do you folks have any opinions about…uhh — about the Messiah's coming?"

Sarah slumped back and rolled her eyes at Simeon. "Oh dear…I see where this is going. Now that you've brought the topic up, we'd better explain to our guests."

She turned to Mother and Father, "My husband has a notion he will live to see the Messiah."

Simeon piped up, "It's more than a notion or a whim. I'd call it a confident hopefulness. I believe that the Lord will actually let me live long enough to see the Promised One."

Sarah shrugged. "Simeon asks all of us the same question week after week: 'Have you heard any news about the Messiah?'"

"And well I should ask. I often wonder how old the Lord will let me get!"

Sarah turned to him and gave him a big kiss on his forehead. "You still feel alive to me. Guess the Messiah isn't here yet."

Mother smiled at the elderly couple's light hearted bantering.

Jediah asked, "Do you mean you really think the Messiah will be born soon?"

Simeon chuckled, "Well, as you can see, I'm not getting any younger!" He grew serious. "Yes, young man. I believe that the Messiah will be born soon. Now back to the first question. Any promising leads this week?"

"Actually — Well, I mean I," stammered Jediah.

A hush came over the room as everyone turned to listen. He took a deep breath and looked earnestly at Simeon. "What would you think if a young couple from Galilee, Nazareth to be specific, were traveling right now to Bethlehem for the census, and knew she would give birth there?"

Simeon thought a moment, choosing his words carefully, and asked slowly, "Do you mean a couple, from the House of David, will give birth to a baby in the city of Bethlehem...perhaps a son, and plan to raise him in Galilee?"

He looked intently at Jediah to emphasize his next question. "Does this couple exist?"

Jediah felt Father flash him a look that meant, "You shouldn't have spoken."

Father stepped in quickly before Jediah began to answer. "I'm sorry, Simeon. I hope my boy didn't get your hopes up. It's true. The old prophecies do fit a certain couple we happen to know, but they're just ordinary, poor people and…"

Simeon interrupted. "So this couple does exist."

Levi spluttered, "Well, yes but…"

Simeon jumped up and clapped. "This is the best news I've had in months! It sounds promising."

Levi forced a crooked smile and shrugged. "Well, Simeon, although I doubt this baby will be the Messiah, I hope you're right. I hope it's soon. I can't wait for him to come and free us from these Romans."

Simeon rubbed a finger slowly back and forth across his chin, pausing to think before responding.

"Well now, I've had my troubles, just like everyone else, with those Roman scoundrels, but don't set your hopes on some kind of a warrior Messiah. He may surprise us and be unlike anything that we expect."

Travel Guide to the Past

- The Hebrew expression Sarah used to greet her family, "Erov Tov" is translated "Good evening."

- The word "Gethsemane" means "olive press," and in the middle of this huge garden was a press for the many olives grown on the slopes. As an adult, Jesus would come here often to pray, and it was here that he would be betrayed and handed over to the temple guards.

- Many Jewish people, at the time of Jesus, believed that the Messiah would come from the East, passing through the Mount of Olives on his triumphant arrival at the Temple.

20. THE HILLS OF BETHLEHEM

JEDIAH AND HIS FAMILY STAYED WITH SIMEON and Sarah for the Sabbath and left the following morning. Bethlehem was a good six miles from Jerusalem. Jediah would never forget the walk to the Temple yesterday when Simeon gave him a prayer shawl. He could still imagine the warmth and weight of the shawl when Simeon placed it on his shoulders. He smiled as he thought of their discussions about the Messiah — knowing he shared the same hope with Simeon of seeing the Messiah soon.

Now as he walked, Jediah opened the bag holding the shawl and touched the fine white wool with the vibrant blue stripe. He dug deeper until he fingered the long blue tassel attached to the edge of the shawl. "Wait till my friends see this," Jediah gloated as he imagined their reaction. He closed the bag as a sudden gust of wind came without warning.

Father pointed to the sky darkened with angry clouds. "Hurry. We're almost there. Let's try to get over these hills into Bethlehem before it rains."

A crash of thunder boomed and the cloud tore open, letting sheets of rain pour down.

"Jediah, run ahead to the caves. We'll meet you there," Father yelled as he stopped to help Eliana with her sandal that had come loose.

Jediah turned and took off, quickly heading in the direction Father pointed. He followed a path that wound its way across the field and down the hill to a row of caves along its edge. Jediah paused, wondering which cave Father meant but quickly decided to run to the opening of the largest.

Jediah was drenched from head to toe. Now the cool air of the cave made him shiver. He took off his wet cloak, shook out his hair, and rubbed the goose bumps on his arms. Peering out of the cave's opening, he watched for his family, but the rain was as heavy as a woolen veil. He didn't see any sign of them.

The wind shifted and blew the wetness in toward him. Jediah moved deeper into the darkness of the cave. He cautiously inched his way along, groping the damp stone walls. He walked into a large cobweb that stuck to his wet face. Jediah stepped aside and bumped his knee on a stone jutting out from the wall.

His groaning stopped short when he heard a noise coming from the deeper part of the cave.

Too scared to back away and too scared to move forward, he stood absolutely still. He stared into the shadows listening, hardly daring to take a breath. It sounded like feet shuffling and soft murmurings coming from the far corner of the cave. His heart began to pound. The coolness of the cave sank deep into his body. Squinting intensely through the darkness, Jediah saw something terrifying: the outline of a man.

A strong fist quickly plunged out of nowhere, grabbing Jediah's wrist, pulling him into the blackness. Jediah fought feverishly to get free, twisting his arm and turning his body to break away from the man's grip.

"Who are you?" snarled the man. His icy words echoed off the stone walls sending a chill through Jediah's bones. A sudden flash of lightning, for a brief moment, revealed the dim outline of the man's head.

Jediah squirmed and shoved the man with all of his might until they both fell against the damp wall. Still the man held on.

Jediah pleaded, "Let me go! Let me go."

"What's your name?" demanded the man.

Jediah gulped hard and stuttered, "Je— Jediah."

Jediah pinched his eyes shut as he felt the man lean in to look at his face. The stranger's warm breath made Jediah shiver. Suddenly the man chuckled and released his grip. Jediah turned to run but stopped when he heard a familiar voice from his past.

"Jediah, is it really you?"

Hardly believing his ears, he called out, "Uncle Avner?"

Avner gave Jediah a big bear hug. "My favorite nephew — I thought you were a thief. There has been trouble with thieves posing as travelers. I figured anyone hiding in this dark cave was up to no good."

Avner felt dampness seeping through from Jediah' wet clothes. He stepped back, holding Jediah at arms length, "You're soaked to the bone! Let's start a fire to warm you up."

Jediah hadn't noticed it before, but hidden near the back of the cave was a small wooden door. It burst open and a boy rushed out.

"Isaac!" Jediah squealed as he dashed over to his cousin.

"Jediah, I thought you might be here. Well, not exactly here, in the cave, but I was hoping we'd see you somewhere in Bethlehem."

Jediah laughed, "We got caught in the storm and Father told me to run to the cave but there are so many. I went to the wrong one."

Isaac grinned. "No! You went to the right one — our cave!"

Avner explained, "Yes. Did your father tell you that this cave belongs to our family?"

Jediah shook his head.

"Well, your father and I had many adventures exploring this cave when we were your age. We'd sit around a fire and listen to your grandfather tell some great stories about King David and how he used this cave as a stable when he was a young shepherd boy."

Jediah spoke with awe. "Imagine, King David in this very spot."

The rain continued to pour down outside as they all sat around the warm fire; a happy family reunion filled with laughter and talking.

Avner apologized to Jediah. "I'm sorry about scaring you earlier. You've grown stronger since we last saw you. Have you been working with your father?"

Jediah nodded.

"You're pretty good at wrestling. The way you were fighting, I figured you must be guilty of something. I was convinced you really were a thief."

Jediah chuckled, "Well this wouldn't be the first time on the journey I was mistaken for a thief. Wait until I tell you about what happened to me at Jericho when some Roman soldiers thought I stole a medal!"

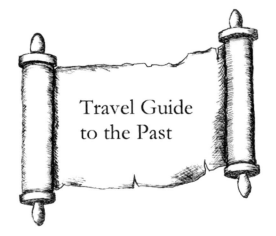

Travel Guide to the Past

• The prayer shawl was worn for prayer at home and at worship in the synagogue. The shawls were white with a stripe of blue near the edges. The vibrant blue dye was expensive because it took thousands of sea snails to obtain enough dye to make the stripe. In ancient times only kings wore garments made of blue. This is why we have the name "royal blue" — only royalty could afford to have enough blue dye for an entire garment. The modern day Israeli flag is designed after the white and blue pattern of the ancient prayer shawls.

• There are hundreds of caves outside the city of Bethlehem. As a young shepherd boy, King David most likely used these caves to stable his flock.

• "Beit Lechem" is the Hebrew name for Bethlehem. It means the House of Bread and foreshadows Jesus, the Bread of Life.

21. CENSUS IN BETHLEHEM

THE STORM BLEW OVER AS QUICKLY AS IT HAD come. Avner noticed the sky lighten and stepped out of the cave. He called back to the boys, "Come on. The rain stopped. Let's go find your family, Jediah!"

They were making their way along a wet, slippery path when Jediah heard Eliana's little voice. "Jediah, I was so worried about you!"

She ran up and squeezed her small arms around his waist.

Jediah gently patted her shoulders and said, "Eliana, I'm all right! You can let go of me. I'm not going anywhere."

By now, Father and Mother caught up to the group. Father rushed forward when he saw his younger brother. "Avner, it's great to see you!"

Avner grinned broadly as Father came near, "It's so good to see you, big brother!"

Eliana pointed at Uncle Avner and Isaac, "Why are you here?"

"Don't I get a hug? A hug before I answer any questions," said Avner.

Eliana nestled into his arms as he answered, "We've come for the census, just like you, but we had a much shorter distance to travel. We left yesterday."

Isaac added, "It only takes a day to get here from Ein Kerem."

Avner and Father looked at each other and said at the same time, "If all goes well and the donkey's fed!"

Father asked Avner, "Where's the rest of your family?"

"We thought it best for Miriam to stay home with the other children. The trip would have been too much for the younger ones."

Mother looked down and pressed her lips together in disappointment. Jediah knew Mother had missed Miriam and talked about her often.

"Two years!" Mother threw her arms up as she exclaimed, "Two years since we have seen you and Miriam!" Mother pushed her hands onto her hips and turned to Father. "Why haven't we come sooner?"

Avner smiled wryly. "Well, that's what happens when you marry a big-shot carpenter. He moves away from his family to where all the work is!" Avner asked Father, "How is Zippori? I hear it's really growing."

Father's grin went from ear to ear, "Is it ever. You should see it!"

Father changed the subject. "Avner, we can talk more about it later but now let's head into Bethlehem and find a place to get settled for the night."

Avner's smile disappeared. "Well, Levi, our hometown, Bethlehem, isn't what it used to be... I mean, Isaac and I already tried to go into town earlier, but they have soldiers stationed at the gate. Nobody gets in without a token, and nobody gets a token until they register at David's house."

Levi shrugged. "Okay. Let's go register."

He turned to take off when Avner quickly grabbed his arm and held him back. "Wait, Levi. There's more to it than just registering." The serious look on Avner's face made everyone stop. "They want us to take an oath swearing to be faithful to Caesar. Anyone who refuses is considered guilty of treason. King Herod is suspicious of anyone who can trace his ancestry to the royal line of King David. That's why they've targeted Bethlehem."

Father stared down at the path, rubbing his brow. "I have to think about this. You know my opinion about the Romans...and Herod is just as bad, but I'm not ready to be part of a rebellion against the government either." He shook his head in disgust and muttered under his breath, "I wish I had faith like old Simeon to believe that the Messiah is coming soon."

Avner spoke firmly, "Levi. We have to deal with this census today. We have to decide now."

Isaac and Jediah anxiously watched their fathers, knowing a wrong decision would be dangerous for them and the whole family.

Levi took a big breath as he reasoned, "It's true. I am not planning to join in a rebellion. I'm not the type of person who would use violence, but I don't like the idea of taking the oath either. It's an insult to us as Jews, but yet, I can in good conscience say I am not planning to undermine the government." He shook his head and sighed deeply, "All right. I can take the oath."

Avner clapped his arm around Father's shoulders and said, "Well, let's go and get it over with."

Together they walked toward Bethlehem. On the outskirts of the city, they came to a large house. There was a continuous stream of people coming in and going out of the building while others gathered in the courtyard to wait.

Father proudly pointed to the house, "This is the childhood home of King David and since we are of his family line, it is, in a way, our family home too."

Jediah and Isaac stared with awe at the ancient structure.

"Does that make me a royal princess?" Eliana asked excitedly, bouncing on her toes.

Mother stroked Eliana's hair. "You're our very own princess — ours alone."

Eliana smiled smugly, satisfied with that answer.

Mother and Eliana waited with the other women in the courtyard as Isaac and Jediah joined their fathers and went into the house. Only the men were required to register for the census. Jewish high priests with solemn faces stood just inside the door, watching to make sure each man paid taxes to support Temple restorations. Soldiers tramped throughout the house keeping an eye out for any troublemakers.

Isaac nudged Jediah with an elbow and pointed to the scrolls heaped upon the table and stuffed into the shelves. "Hope they can find our fathers' names," he whispered.

When they came to the front of the line, the man sitting behind the table called out impatiently, "Next. Hurry up."

One of the soldiers growled at Father and Avner. "Yes you. You're next."

They stepped forward.

"Where are you from?"

Jediah and Isaac watched as he rummaged through the scrolls and found the right scrolls for Levi and Avner. They each signed the census record and the man barked, "Now, move down there to recite the oath."

Jediah watched as Father hesitated for a just a moment before taking a deep breath and continuing.

After they paid their taxes, the soldier at the door gave them a small token, "Don't lose this. You'll need it to enter the city gate."

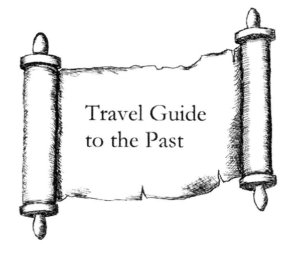

Travel Guide to the Past

- Although there were no wars going on in the Roman Empire at the time of Christ's birth, there were conflicts between the Jews and Romans in the city of Jerusalem and the surrounding areas. The Jewish historian, Josephus, recorded that in 4 BC, a riot in Jerusalem at the Passover Feast resulted in the massacre of 3000 people.

- A census had a history of triggering uprisings. Most Jews, like Levi, considered it an insult to be counted as part of the Roman Empire. They thought of themselves as belonging to Yahweh alone.

- Isaac and Jediah's fathers had to pay three taxes when they registered in Bethlehem. The first tax went to the Roman rulers, the second tax went to Jewish officials to pay off the debt from Temple restorations, and the third tax was meant for widows and the poor.

22. The Market in Bethlehem

It was late afternoon by the time they finished registering at the census building and entered the town of Bethlehem. They all went directly to the family house. Father's relative, Nathan, answered the door. "Levi! Avner! Good to see you. Are you looking for a place to stay? Right now the house is full but, if you don't mind, you're welcome to sleep on my upper patio."

Father and Avner gladly accepted his hospitality, relieved to have a safe place for their families to stay. Isaac and Jediah raced each other up the stone stairs to see where they would be sleeping.

"We get to sleep under the stars!" Isaac said.

Jediah added, "This is going to be fun."

Nathan brought up the bedding as they unpacked. That evening they ate dinner with family they hadn't seen for years, and visited late into the night before settling in for bed.

The next morning Jediah's family walked to the market. Jediah asked, "I wonder where Joseph and Mary are. Do you think they're in Bethlehem yet?"

"Oh, I forgot to tell you," Father said. "Mary and Joseph are having a hard time finding a place to stay. They stopped by early this morning and Isaac took them to see if Bartholomew had any room."

"How does Isaac know Joseph and Mary?" Jediah interrupted.

Father laughed. "Well, apparently we're not the only ones who know Joseph and Mary. Isaac and his family spent quite some time with Mary several months ago when she stayed in Ein Kerem with Zachariah and Elizabeth. Let's keep an eye out for them."

Arella added, "Imagine; two cousins, who live so far away both knowing Mary and Joseph."

They walked through the winding, narrow dirt roads, past the small homes of Bethlehem and came to the central marketplace. Mother began bargaining with one of the local merchants when Eliana spotted Isaac with Mary and Joseph.

She shouted, "There they are!"

Mary and Joseph looked tired; their faces weary; their clothes rumpled. After talking a short while, Mary joined Mother and Eliana to look for a few things in the market.

When the women were out of earshot, Father asked, "Any luck at finding a place to stay?"

Joseph grimaced and rubbed the back of his neck as he confided, "During this whole journey, I've been assuring my new wife that we would have family to stay with in Bethlehem, and we would have a good place to settle in for the baby to be born. Otherwise, I would have never let her come. I would have insisted she stay home with her mother!"

Father slowly replied, "So, I assume all of your relatives…"

"Full," Joseph interrupted, throwing his arms up as he talked. "Their homes are full! We've been to seven homes now, and they have nothing to offer us. Levi, I don't know what we're going to do. The only place Isaac and I found to stay is in a corner of the courtyard by the Census building. That won't work and we don't have much time."

Jediah felt bad for Joseph. He knew Mary would need someplace private to have the baby. Suddenly he had an idea. "Father, could Joseph and Mary stay in the cave where I met Avner and Isaac?"

Father turned to Joseph, "Jediah has a good idea. It's nothing special, just an old family cave, but it is dry and warm and it's yours for as long as you want."

Joseph's face lifted, "Well, it's not exactly what I was hoping for, but it's the best possibility I've come across so far. I'll talk it over with Mary." He patted Father's shoulder and ran over to catch up with Mary.

Father watched at a distance as the young couple discussed Jediah's idea of staying in the cave. He saw Mary smile and Joseph's face relax. Joseph looked back and nodded.

Father asked Jediah and Isaac, "Can you boys remember how to get to the cave?"

They looked at each other, "Sure."

"Good. Then you bring Joseph, and help him get the cave fixed up. When Mary and Mother finish at the market, they'll meet you there later. I'll take Eliana back to Nathan's house."

Isaac and Jediah brought Joseph to the cave. Now as they looked at it in broad daylight, they found it was dirtier than they remembered. Jediah felt embarrassed as they showed it to Joseph. The cave stunk like animals and was full of dirty hay and cobwebs. Joseph took a thorough assessment of the cave, knowing this was the only option left for them. He rolled up the sleeves of his tunic and said, "I think we can make it work, but I'll need your help. It'll take all of our sweat and muscle to get it ready."

The three of them worked hard pulling out stashes of old hay, swiping dusty cobwebs from the corners, and sweeping the floors. Joseph looked around, satisfied with their progress.

Isaac asked, "What about the room in the back of the cave? Shouldn't we clean it too?"

Joseph looked around puzzled, "What room? I don't see any room."

Isaac laughed, "It's hidden around the corner of that big rock. I've been back there once but it was dark."

The back room was larger than the front cave and in pretty good shape. Joseph discovered a couple large rugs rolled up along a wall, a small table with two lanterns, and fresh hay.

"It looks like people may have stayed here off and on throughout the years. This table is rickety, but I can fix that. Could you boys shake out the rugs?"

Joseph went to work fixing the table. Next he took on the job of cleaning a stone manger which hung on the cave's wall about a foot high off the floor.

When the boys came back from shaking the rugs, they watched him carefully pick up every last bit of dirty straw from the manger and rub the inside of it clean with a cloth.

"Why are you cleaning that?" Isaac asked.

"Well, it might come in handy for the baby. Back in Nazareth, I had made a crib, but we couldn't bring it along on the trip. Maybe this will do for the baby until we go back home."

By the time Mother and Mary arrived, Joseph and the boys had finished. Isaac and Jediah stood at the front opening, with proud grins on their faces, watching the two women enter. It was still a stable but provided the shelter and privacy they needed. It smelled of sweet hay and was warmed by a glowing fire.

Mary looked at the boys. "Thank you, for helping to make this so clean and cozy for us and the baby.

Mother and Mary had bargained well at the market and found everything the young couple needed to stay for a while. As they unpacked their purchases, Mary spoke to Joseph, "Arella has offered to help when the baby is born... if that's alright with you."

Joseph looked relieved. "Thank you, Arella. I'm afraid I wouldn't be much help."

Mother laughed, "Oh, there'll still be plenty for you to do. I'll depend on your help to get fresh water from the stream and a nice fire for boiling it. When the time comes, run to Nathan's house to get me. It's the second house just over the hill on the edge of town. I'll take care of the rest."

Mother turned to Jediah and Isaac, "We should get going back to Nathan's now. They'll be looking for us. Let's give Joseph and Mary time to settle in and get some rest."

Travel Guide
to the Past

▪ The gospel of Luke tells us that Mary and Joseph ended up staying in a stable where animals were kept. The bible does not elaborate on how Mary and Joseph came about finding the stable — but Bethlehem is surrounded by hundreds of natural caves that were used by shepherds over the ages to shelter their flocks.

23. Nathan's House

A FEW DAYS LATER, DURING THE EVENING meal, a sharp rap-rap-rap sounded on the door. Nathan opened it to find Joseph standing there pale and out of breath. "Mary said it's time for the baby! Is Arella here?"

Mother jumped up from the dinner mat and wiped her hands. "I'm right here, Joseph. Let me grab a few things and I'll come with you."

Jediah and Isaac were excited knowing that the baby was on the way. They each secretly wondered if it would be a boy, and if he would be the Messiah.

After they finished eating, it was late, and the men sent the children to bed up on the rooftop. Eliana drifted easily to sleep but the anticipation about Mary's baby kept Jediah and Isaac from settling down. There was much on their minds and they stayed wide awake whispering to each other.

The sky was dark, when Isaac noticed something brilliant and unearthly.

"Hey look at that," he said, pointing to the east. "Over there — just outside of town. Do you see it?"

A strange glowing brightness danced in the sky. At times the brilliant light circled around and fluttered.

"What is it? It's over by the shepherds' hills," Jediah said.

The boys rested on their backs watching the brightness flash and dance in the sky.

Below them, in the walled courtyard, the men were talking in animated voices. The boys rolled onto their bellies and inched their way over to the edge of the patio to listen.

They heard Nathan say, "The Romans around here have been on edge over this census. They're afraid of another uprising. And Herod has his own secret police spying on us."

Nathan glanced over his shoulder and continued in a lowered voice. "He's afraid someone from the line of David will challenge him to the throne. We're targets. Believe me. You don't want to mention the word 'messiah' out on the streets."

Isaac looked, wide-eyed at Jediah, "Can I tell you a secret?"

Jediah propped his face in his hands to listen as Isaac began talking, "I told you about Mary visiting in Ein Kerem, but I didn't tell you the whole story."

Isaac told Jediah about all of the strange things that had happened this year; Zachariah seeing an angel and loosing his voice; elderly Elizabeth having a baby, he paused, "And I never told you the story of Mary." Isaac whispered, "She said an angel had told her she would give birth to the Messiah."

He stopped for a moment and carefully watched Jediah's reaction. "Do you think it could be true, Jediah? Do you think it's possible that Mary's baby is the Messiah?"

Jediah replied emphatically, "I have some stories to tell you too. One night along the journey, we were talking about the Messiah and realized all the prophecies fit Mary and Joseph perfectly. That's got to be more than just a coincidence. Plus when we brought this up, Joseph's face turned red and he looked away, like he was hiding a secret."

Isaac's eyes lit up. "See! See it could be true."

Jediah added, "Wait. There's more. When we were in Jerusalem, I met a wise old priest named Simeon, the one who gave me the shawl. He said that the Lord told him that the Messiah will be born soon. In fact, he insisted that the Lord promised he would let him live to see the Messiah. And believe me it must be soon, because he is very, very old already."

The boys stopped talking when they heard loud pounding. The banging sounded as if it might break Nathan's door.

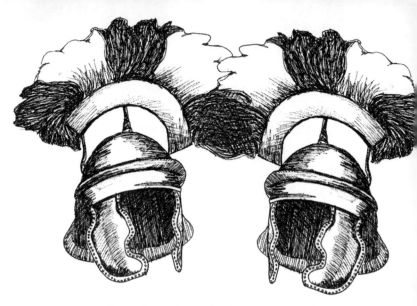

At first they thought it was Joseph again and peeked over the ledge of the roof. They ducked down when they saw two Roman soldiers standing there.

Nathan's voice had an edge to it. "Yes?"

One of the soldiers huffed, "Now, don't get defensive, Nathan. We have a couple questions. Your wife had a baby not long ago, didn't she? Was it a son? Is he the one all this nonsense is about?"

Jediah and Isaac listened as Nathan's voice grew irritated and he snapped back, "Titus, I don't know what you're talking about. I had a baby girl, Anna. And who's talking nonsense?"

Titus rebuffed, "Don't pretend you don't know. Some of your friends, the shepherds, just came into town from the fields ranting and raving about some light they had seen from angels floating in the sky. Their story is that the angels sang and told them a baby boy was born who will free them. That's enough to cause an uprising. And we're going to find this baby and get to the bottom of it before word of it gets to Herod. We thought it might be you."

Nathan denied knowing anything about the story the soldiers were telling.

"Don't think you're off the hook. We know you've spend a lot of time with those shepherds. Were you with them earlier tonight? What kind of prank are they pulling?"

Nathan squared his shoulders and glared as he gave the Romans an answer. "My house is full, as you can see. I've been busy here with family. And as far as my shepherd friends — they're good people, whatever you may think of them. We've pulled a few fast ones on each other before, but I know they wouldn't joke about something like the Messiah's birth."

The other soldier barked, "Come on Titus. Let's keep checking around."

Titus looked intently at Nathan and warned, "We're going to keep an eye on you. I don't trust you."

Jediah and Isaac looked at each other. Now they knew that the light they had seen must have been the angels the shepherds were talking about. The two boys scurried back to their sleeping mats, putting their heads together, analyzing everything they had found out about the Messiah.

Finally, Jediah cleared his throat, "Okay. So we've decided we're certain of two things."

Isaac shook his head up and down, his eyes sparkling with excitement.

"First, Joseph and Mary's newborn baby must be the Messiah. And secondly," Jediah paused, almost afraid to say it, "secondly, that he was born tonight — and my mother was there!"

Both boys stopped talking and froze as they heard footsteps coming up the stairs. It was their fathers.

"Don't pretend to be sleeping, you two. We know you've been awake this whole time."

Levi and Avner sat down next to them, "Have you figured it out like we have?"

The boys nodded excitedly. Isaac burst out in a loud whisper, "Yes! Joseph, Mary, the Messiah—everything!"

Levi rested his hands on each of their heads, "We're fortunate to be living in these times and we're even more blessed to know what has happened tonight."

Avner broke in with a warning, "But you must not tell anyone. It would be very dangerous for Joseph and Mary if the soldiers found out that they have a newborn baby. We have to warn them about the soldiers and help them get whatever they need so they can stay hidden for a few days." He looked at Father, "Levi, how are we all going to get out of the house and past those Romans without them following us?"

176

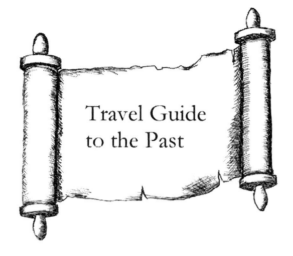

Travel Guide
to the Past

- King Herod was appointed by the Romans. He ruled from 37 BC up to 4 BC. Judean citizens disliked him because he did not follow Jewish customs or laws and imposed excessive taxes. Herod was suspicious of anyone whom he thought might try to take away his kingdom. He was especially disturbed about any news of a messiah coming from the royal line of David.

- Herod stationed soldiers in Bethlehem and throughout Judea. They acted as secret police were known to use violence to enforce order.

- It was customary for a woman to give birth in her mother's home but since Mary was far away from her family when her time was due, a midwife from Bethlehem or a woman who knew her may have been there to help.

24. THE CAVE IN BETHLEHEM

HUNDREDS OF STARS DOTTED THE NIGHT SKY over Bethlehem. It would still be a few hours before they would fade with early dawn. Father scooped up Eliana from her bed as she mumbled, "The balsam, get the balsam!" Father handed her the small cloth bag with the sweet fragrance. Eliana clenched it in her fingers as she wrapped her arms around Father's neck.

Avner motioned for the boys to follow, and led them down the stairs quietly so they wouldn't wake the rest of the household.

He whispered, "Be careful. There's a lot at stake!"

Isaac's heart beat faster as his father explained, "We have to stay hidden. Those Romans have been watching Nathan's house. They're suspicious he may have something to do with the shepherds' commotion last night. If they see us leave, they might follow us and we would lead them right to Joseph and Mary, and the Messiah!"

Father added, "For now, the Romans don't believe the shepherds' story, but they're trying to figure it all out. We don't want to give them any more clues. Herod is a jealous king and it would be very dangerous for Mary and Joseph if he heard of the Messiah's birth. We have to warn them to keep hidden."

Avner suggested, "We should go the back roads around Bethlehem to avoid being seen by the soldiers. Follow close and be quiet!"

Father leaned out the door and looked carefully to make sure the street was empty.

"Come on," he whispered.

They darted along buildings, moving from shadow to shadow, trying not to make any sound that would get the soldiers' attention.

Isaac, at the end of the line, looked back from time to time to make sure they were not being followed.

Suddenly Father stopped and motioned for the rest to come closer, deeper into the shadows. He pointed: soldiers. The quiet darkness was pierced as the Romans spoke.

"I know how unreliable shepherds are, but we can't stop looking. We need to find this baby, if he does exist, and ... Shh. I hear something."

Jediah froze as the soldier took a step toward them; the soldier's eyes scanning for any movement.

"Did he see us?" Jediah worried.

The soldier paused and then threw his hands up in the air. "It's ridiculous for us to be hunting for a baby in the middle of the night, but if word of this should get to King Herod, he would be furious. Let's keep an eye on Nathan. He seems to know more than he's telling us."

The soldiers turned off toward Nathan's house.

Father gave a quick flick of his hand, signaling them to follow quickly. It wasn't until they slipped though the city gates, away from the soldiers, that Jediah finally relaxed his shoulders in relief.

Isaac whispered to Jediah as they walked along the rocky path. "That was scary, wasn't it?"

Jediah nodded.

Father softly chuckled and spoke to Avner, "This brings back memories of that night when we were boys and snuck out together during the Passover Feast. Do you remember how scared we were?" Both fathers snickered as they reminisced about the old days. Their laughter died down as they came near the caves.

"Here we are," said Avner. "Everyone move in quickly."

As Father set Eliana down she looked around the cave. Seeing only the dark outer room, she tugged on Jediah's sleeve.

"No one's here!"

"They're in a back room. See that tiny bit of light in the corner? That's the door."

Isaac added, "It's the perfect hiding spot for them. Even if you knew it was here, it's hard to spot."

Jediah and Isaac led the way to the small wooden door. They paused for a split second before entering. They knew that behind it lay the hopes and dreams of thousands of people— the Messiah, their savior!

"Are you ready?" asked Avner, as he nudged them toward the door.

They all took a deep breath and stepped in.

Joseph stood up to greet them. "Welcome. You're the second group of visitors we've had since the baby was born. News travels fast!"

Mother rushed over to Father and asked, "Levi, it's the middle of the night. Is something wrong?"

Father sighed deeply. "We're all right, but we had to come in the cover of darkness to warn you, Joseph. The shepherds came into town after seeing the baby, and it caused quite a stir. The Romans are looking for you."

Joseph patted Jediah on the back, "Your idea about this stable has kept us safe. I was so upset when we couldn't stay with my family in town, but now I see how dangerous that would have been. You can't always understand the Lord's plans ahead of time."

Father looked squarely into Joseph's eyes and spoke, "Now, can we see him?"

Joseph smiled, "You know, don't you. I can tell that you've figured out he's the Promised One."

Father nodded, "Yes Joseph. We all had suspicions since our talk around the campfire at the Jordan River. It took us a while to believe something like this could actually happen."

Joseph led them over to a deep pile of hay where Mary was resting with the baby.

She smiled tenderly. "Come, look at him."

They all came closer and gathered around. His tiny mouth opened into a wide yawn.

Mother said, "I think he looks like you, Mary: your nose, your chin, even your eyes."

Mary gently stroked the fine black hair on the top of his head as baby Jesus drifted back to sleep. Jediah felt a tingle move down his spine. He and Isaac knelt down by the infant to get a better look.

Isaac whispered, "He looks like an ordinary baby. Who would ever guess he was so special that an angel announced his coming?"

Jediah became thoughtful and spoke softly, "I'll remember this day for the rest of my life. I have a feeling in my heart — I can't explain it. "

Mary looked at the boys. "I have a favor to ask each of you."

The boys leaned toward Mary to listen.

"Jediah, I need someone to tell my mother that Jesus is born. Would you stop through Nazareth on your way home?"

"Sure," he said as he smiled at Father.

Mary smiled. "Thank you. And Isaac, would you bring the good news to Elizabeth and Zachariah in Ein Kerem?"

"I'll tell them as soon as we get back."

Eliana sat down next to Mary. "I have something for Jesus." She held the bundle of balsam high and gave it a little swing.

Mary opened the bag and a sweet fragrance flooded the room. "Thank you, Eliana. Your mother told me how useful balsam is for babies."

Jediah sat quietly, holding the white woolen prayer shawl that Simeon had given him.

Father asked, "Jediah, why did you bring that along?"

"Last night, I had an idea."

He kissed the corner of the prayer shawl and handed it to Joseph. "I want to give this prayer shawl to your baby. I'm sorry it's not new. It got a little rumpled on the journey but it's one of my favorite things. It was a gift from a holy man, Simeon. You'll meet him when you go to Jerusalem. He's in the Temple every day waiting to see the Messiah." Jediah smiled, looking down at baby Jesus. "And here He is."

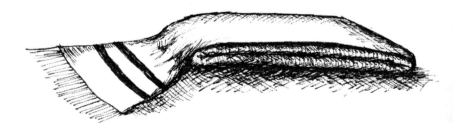

Joseph graciously accepted the shawl and Mary said, "What a wonderful gift. This is a gift that was hard for you to give but those are the most precious."

"Mary," Isaac quietly interrupted. "Mary, I'm sorry. I don't have anything to give."

Mary looked into his eyes and spoke kindly. "Isaac, you have something important to give. It's something you can do for him."

"What's that?"

"Believe. Believe that he's the Messiah — that this tiny baby is the Promised One who has come to save us." Mary looked at all of them and continued. "Today I have the newborn Messiah in my arms, but each of you can carry him in your heart. If you choose to believe in him, he will fill you with joy."

Isaac replied, "I didn't expect the Messiah to be a baby and I didn't expect him to be born in an old cave, or that his first visitors would be shepherds…" His voice trailed off.

After a moment, Isaac looked at Mary and said firmly, "but I do believe. I really believe that he is the Messiah; the one we've been waiting for — the one God sent to save us."

Jediah nudged Isaac, "And to think we're actually here with him in this quiet cave — our Destination: Bethlehem."

BIBLIOGRAPHY

Selected resources used for background information:

•New American Bible. Sacred Scripture and Footnotes

•Cantalamessa, Raniero. Jesus Christ, the Holy One of God. Collegeville, Minn., Liturgical Press, 1991

•Cavins, Jeff. The Great Adventure Bible Timeline Series. Ascension Press, 2003

•Dorling, K. Jerusalem and the Holy Land. New York, 2000

•Edersheim, Alfred. Sketches of Jewish Social Life

•Emmerich, Bl Anne Catherine. The Life of the Blessed Virgin Mary. Tan Books, Rockford, Ill., 2004

•Filas, Fr. Francis L. St. Joseph and Daily Christian Living. The Macmillan Co., 1959

•Hahn, Scott. Hail Holy Queen. Doubleday Co., 2001

•Pope John Paul II. The Person and Mission of St Joseph in the Life of Christ and of the Church, 1989

•Ray, Steven. Jesus: The Word Became Flesh DVD. Ignatius Press & St. Joseph Productions, 2004
•Time-Life Books. The Holy Land, Alexandria, Va. c1992.
•Tvedtnes, John. Bedouin Culture and Customs. 1970
•Wright, Tom. The Original Jesus. Erdman Publishing Co., Grand Rapids, MI, 1997

Websites used for background information:

•African Wildlife Foundation. www.afw/jackals.com
•Ein Kerem. www.netours.com/jrs/2003/Ein-Kerem
•Ein Kerem. www.thinkeilat.com
•Gethsemane. www.biblehistory.com/jerusalem
•Houses of Ancient Israel. www.fas.harvard.edu
•Medjugorje. www.medjugorje.org/olmmsg
•Mount Gilboa. www.ancientsandals.com/
•Hebrew www.headcoverings-by-Devorah.com
•Jericho. www.bibleplaces.com
•Jewish Priests. www.answers.com/topic/kohen
•Shofar. www.jewishvirtuallibrary.org/jsource
•Lambing FAQ. www.sheepscreek.com
•Roman Military Equipment www.romanlegions.info
•The Holy Land and the Bible. www.Philologos.org
•The Second Temple. www.newadvent.org
•The Second Temple. www.ust.ucla.edu/ustweb/israel
•Valley Gate, Jerusalem. www.pilgrimtours.com/Isracl
•Zippori. www.jewishvirtuallibrary.org
•Zippori. www.zipori.com

CPSIA information can be obtained at www.ICGtesting.com
Printed in the USA
BVOW04s2223121114

374765BV00001B/11/P